BLAKE'S SEVEN

Terry Nation's
BLAKE'S SEVEN
Scorpio Attack

a novel by
TREVOR HOYLE
based on the scripts written by
Chris Boucher
James Follett
Robert Holmes

CITADEL PRESS
Secaucus, New Jersey

Published 1988 by Citadel Press
A division of Lyle Stuart Inc.
120 Enterprise Ave., Secaucus, N.J. 07094
In Canada: Musson BookCompany
A division of General Publishing Co. Limited
Don Mills, Ontario

By arrangement with BBC Books
A division of BBC Enterprises Ltd.

Format copyright © 1981 by Lynstead Park Enterprises Limited
Novelization copyright © 1981 by Trevor Hoyle
All rights reserved.

Manufactured in the United States of America
ISBN 0-8065-1082-X

Contents

Part One *Rescue* 7
Part Two *Traitor* 57
Part Three *Stardrive* 109

PART ONE
RESCUE

Chapter One

'There's something moving down there.'

Avon raised the magni-viewer to his eyes and pressed the zoom control. There was a soft whirring sound. The field of vision narrowed and the 3-D image swam into life-size close-up. When the whirring stopped the focus had sharpened automatically to crystal clarity.

Something odd about that ship, just sitting down there on the snow-covered plain. Through the viewer it looked innocent enough. Too damned innocent. Avon frowned and gnawed his lower lip.

Lying beside him in the harsh reedlike grass, legs splayed, Dayna cradled the snub-nosed high-velocity projectile weapon under her chin. 'Servalan told us it was an old ship.'

'It's what she didn't tell us that interests me.' Avon panned slowly along the curved metal hull and spotted movement near the open airlock. Sunlight glinted on a thermoplastic dome with stubby flexible extensors: the maintenance Link trundled about doing routine tasks.

Avon relaxed slightly. 'It's just a Link. Heading for the main lock.'

He watched the animal turn jerkily, about to enter the airlock. Then it came to him. *Of course——*

Avon ducked and yanked Dayna's arm. 'Get down! Cover your eyes!'

There was a blinding white flash, eerily silent, followed by a buffeting shockwave as the force of the explosion hit them like a solid brick wall. Snow, small rocks and chunks of metal rained down.

When it had cleared Dayna raised her head to look. Avon

didn't bother. He squirmed round to sit up, and said crisply, 'So much for what Servalan didn't tell us.'

Wide-eyed, Dayna said, 'Quite a booby-trap.'

'Half a booby-trap to be exact.' Avon took the weapon from her and stood up. 'Come on, let's go.'

'Half a booby-trap?'

'You don't imagine Servalan would mine the ship and leave the living quarters intact?' Avon lifted an eyebrow, as if it pained him to state so obvious a fact. Behind that lean, sardonic, rather brutal face it was impossible to know whether he felt alarmed or even remotely concerned that the rest of the crew might be in mortal danger.

Dayna sprang to her feet. 'We've got to warn the others!'

'Take it slowly, Dayna.'

'Slowly?' The black girl halted in mid-stride and whirled round. She was a magnificent looking woman, lithe and graceful, with a generous figure that even the crumpled combat suit couldn't hide. Dust layered her short black hair, which was razor-cut so that it outlined the shape of her head.

Avon said patiently, 'It's going to be no help to them if we walk into something hungry on the way back.'

'I don't intend to *walk* into anything,' she told him curtly, starting up the steep slope. Avon caught her arm and swung her round.

'Don't be stupid.'

'Let me go, Avon.'

He looked into her face for a moment, seeing the firm set of her mouth. Then gave the smallest of shrugs and relaxed his hold.

'I'll see you back at the base,' Dayna called over her shoulder.

Avon didn't look up from checking the weapon. 'I doubt it.'

Dayna skirted some rocks and loped through the sparse undergrowth. She'd never understand what went on in that computer brain of his. She was flesh and blood, an emotional creature, and she expected others to be the same. Didn't he *care* about the others? Here they were, stranded on a hunk of rock and scrub called Terminal, their ship *Liberator* destroyed, with one functioning weapon between the five of them (six if you counted Orac, which she didn't), and Avon behaved as if they were vacationing on a paradise planet. No sense of urgency. No sense of loyalty to his fellow——

A raucous high-pitched gibbering scream brought her skidding to a halt, the toes of her tightly-laced combat boots digging into the snow-covered undergrowth.

Dayna's heart and stomach changed places. She crouched, arms spread, staring at a bush with broad leathery leaves being violently shaken. Something had just been killed and eaten. By something bigger that she had no wish to encounter. Maybe if she was very, very careful and quiet, the big something might not know she was there and let her alone.

She was wrong on both counts. The creature knew she was there and it was hungry for more.

Dayna's mouth opened soundlessly wide as a long green scaly neck suddenly writhed snake-like into the air, oval black eyes and pointed fangs dripping blood turning in her direction. The smooth black snout picked up her heat-scent. The elongated head seemed to grin, and then it swooped towards her.

Dayna stumbled backwards. Her eyes went glassy with terror. It was so quick she couldn't believe it. She thrust out her hands to ward it off, the heel of her boot struck a rock, and she slipped and fell, instinctively drawing up her knees as the scaly green head lunged for her, saliva dripping redly from its jaws.

She tried to scream but couldn't. The hairs on her spine stood up like stiff bristles. She could hear and smell its foul wheezing breath.

Less than three feet away, the creature's head exploded.

Dayna jerked as if she too had been shot, and cowered back with sick loathing as she watched the headless ragged neck whipping the air before falling in a twitching coil, oozing green slime. Bits of the head lay scattered around. The stench was obscene.

Avon ejected the spent high-velocity shell and came through the scrub towards her. 'Are you ready to take it slowly now?' he asked, his eyes hooded, his face impassive.

Dayna climbed shakily to her feet. 'Don't you ever get bored, Avon,' she wanted to know, sucking in a deep breath, 'with being right all the time?'

'Just with the rest of you being wrong.' There was no hint of irony; he was perfectly serious. Avon unslung the viewer from around his neck and tossed it to her. 'Try and keep a sharp look-out. We can't afford to waste any more ammunition.'

Waste! Saving her life! Dayna glared at him but bit her tongue. After all . . . he *had* been right. She looked at the mangled seeping neck on the ground and turned away, shuddering. She said, 'If you're also right about the base——'

'If I'm right about the base, then the charges will already have been triggered,' Avon told her calmly.

Dayna paused, about to slip the strap over her head. 'What do you mean?'

'Ultrasonic fuses keyed to pick up the explosion of the ship. That's how I'd have done it,' he said, as if this were merely an academic problem they were discussing.

'Then they're already dead,' said Dayna numbly.

'That's what we're going to find out.'

And with that he turned, weapon tucked into the crook of his arm, and set off down the slope.

The heavy iron cover was raised an inch or two and thick black smoke billowed out of the shaft. A moment later the cover fell back on its hinges and an arm appeared, clad in a tattered, soot-blackened sleeve. Then Vila's head, his face set in a grimace as he strained to lug the unconscious body of Tarrant out into the fresh air. Considering that Tarrant topped six feet and weighed a hundred and eighty pounds plus, this was no easy task for the smaller, lightly-built man.

'Come on, you great oaf,' Vila grunted. 'This is no time to take a nap.'

From deep underground came the gritty rumble of an explosion. If Vila needed further incentive, that was it. Desperation lending him strength, he hauled Tarrant clear of the shaft and dragged him several yards before collapsing himself in a paroxysm of coughing.

Vila sat up and spat into the sand. 'If I've broken my back hauling a corpse about, I'll never forgive you, Tarrant.'

He leaned across, pressing his ear to Tarrant's chest. His heartbeat was muffled and erratic, but at least he had one. Vila unfastened the big man's collar, and then went very still. He straightened up and glanced towards the shaft. Thick strands of black smoke curled upwards. What the hell was he doing?

Cally!

Staggering back to the shaft, Vila peered in nervously. The smoke was clearing. Had she been the last out when the first explosion went off? He couldn't remember. Anyway, that didn't matter . . . what did was that she was still in there.

'Cally?' He cleared his throat and called louder. 'Cally?'

Vila dithered, put one foot on the iron ladder and took it off again. He was no galactic hero. He'd saved Tarrant, what else did they expect of him? He backed reluctantly away from the shaft, and as he turned a voice, more in his mind than actually audible, uttered an agonised whisper.

V-i-l-a . . .

'Cally?' Not daring to think twice in case he had second thoughts, Vila ran back and climbed into the shaft. 'Hang on, Cally, I'm coming!'

Halfway down he felt the ladder vibrate in his sweating palms as another explosion went off deep below. And then another, louder this time, almost making him slip. And then another, still louder, and yet another.

For a frozen moment Vila hung on as the sequence of explosions marched nearer, like giant footsteps. The ladder was coming away from the wall, the brackets jarred loose from the concrete. He felt it sway perilously and scrambled up as the latest explosion sent a furnace blast of heat past him, almost lifting him bodily out of the shaft. Sprinting away, he flung himself to the ground and covered his head.

A fiery tongue leapt skywards and the ground heaved like something in pain. The explosion seemed to erupt inside his head, and in all the noise and confusion he heard, softly yet distinctly, that familiar telepathic voice at the still epicentre of the raging firestorm spewing from the shaft:

Blake . . . Blake . . . Blake . . .

As the tremulous rumble of explosions died away, so her faint despairing cries faded into silence.

Vila lay still, his finger clutching the earth, his head ringing but empty of words.

Chapter Two

Dorian yawned, rubbed his stubbly chin, and flexed his shoulders. Couldn't be far off now, even at the sub-speeds that were the best this old rusty bucket could attain flat out. One day – and soon – he'd have to get hold of a new main drive unit.

He eased himself out from behind the flight control module and stepped down onto the main deck. Tall, ruggedly handsome, with black glossy hair that hung down to the grimy collar of his rumpled space fatigues, Dorian might have been the personification of the dashing story-book Space Captain had not his appearance been so shabbily disreputable. Yet there was a vestige of truth in it even so as master, mate and crew of the cargo freighter *Scorpio* – all rolled into one.

Hands on hips, Dorian stood in front of the ship's computer, which was nothing more impressive than a panel of tiny multicoloured winking lights set into the bulkhead. It was a standard model he'd installed himself with certain rather special modifications. Including a 'personality' which suited his ironic, offbeat sense of humour. On long flights diversions were doubly welcome.

'Slave?'

'Yes, Master,' responded the mild, obedient voice at once.

'How long before we make planetfall?'

'One hour, Master. That is Earth Standard Time of course.' The computer added obsequiously, 'I hope that is satisfactory.'

Dorian frowned and returned to the flight control module. He punched up a scanner readout. 'There's still no sign of the *Liberator* on our screens.'

It sounded like an accusation.

Had Slave possessed a throat, it might have cleared it anxiously.

'I fear not, Master.'

Dorian punched up more readouts. 'I'm getting a heavy radiation shadow. Focus looks to be on zero-zero-one to our present heading. Check it.'

'At once, Master.' Slave fell silent. Then: 'It appears to be the residual of an explosion, Master. Analysis of the radiation pattern suggests it could have happened near the planet of our destination.'

'And it generated a lot more power than the death of any normal ship would have done,' said Dorian thoughtfully.

'You are correct, as always, Master.'

Dorian raised his head. 'Do you think it was the *Liberator*?'

'Thought is beyond my humble capacities, Master.'

'True. Increase speed by twenty per cent.'

'Yes, Master.'

'Scan for wreckage. Analyse anything associated with the explosion pattern.'

'Of course, Master. I would most respectfully point out, however, that there is unlikely to be anything worth salvaging.'

Dorian's tanned face was stony. 'You're thinking, Slave.'

'I'm sorry, Master. I meant no disrespect.' The tone

15

became wheedling. 'I am your most humble slave, in all——'

'Enough!'

'Yes, Master.'

'I expect a positive identification of the cause of that explosion within the hour, Slave.'

'I will do my poor best.'

'You will indeed.' It was more a threat than a promise. 'If it was the *Liberator* the crew may still be alive, and helpless, down on that planet.'

'A rescue mission, Master?'

'Not exactly, Slave.' Dorian leaned back in the padded seat, the tarnished buttons on his tunic winking dully. His eyes were narrowed; he was brooding. 'Not exactly.'

Purple twilight: a thin spiral of smoke curled lazily from the small campfire on the edge of the clearing. The fire was not only for warmth but for protection. Nightfall on the planet Terminal signalled open season for greedy predators.

Vila piled on more wood and sat watching the flames crackle up and devour it. He shivered. *Devour*. Come on, snap out of it, he chided himself. Think of something that doesn't involve the gastric system. The planet couldn't be entirely populated by empty stomachs; and a mocking reply came instantly from his cynical other self, *Want to bet?*

On the other side of the fire Dayna was bending anxiously over Tarrant, applying a damp cloth to his forehead. To her relief his breathing was easier now, and some colour had returned to his cheeks. His eyelids fluttered open and he struggled to sit up, rubbing his neck.

'What happened?'

'Take it easy,' Dayna soothed him, pressing a slim black hand to his broad shoulder. 'Vila got you out.'

Tarrant shook his head groggily. 'Vila rescued me?'

For the past half hour Avon had been tinkering with Orac, trying to repair it with the few basic tools he carried. It was hopeless. Yet without Orac's superior electronic intelligence they were sunk. The realisation made him short-tempered and more brusque than usual. Without looking up from his task, he said: 'You were injured trying to rescue Cally. Vila rescued you. Suddenly I'm hip-deep in heroes.'

Tarrant sat up properly, glancing round. 'Where *is* Cally?'

Dayna bit her lip and looked towards Vila.

It was Avon who spoke, simply stating a fact. 'Cally's dead.'

'Are you sure?'

'I'm sure.'

'He went back in,' Dayna said.

Tarrant looked at Avon. He said softly, 'You wanted to be a hero too?'

'We needed Orac.' Avon tossed the diagnostic probing device aside in disgust. 'We still do.'

'Orac got a bit dented,' Vila explained. 'For which he blames me. It seems I rescued the wrong one.'

Avon looked at Tarrant for the first time. 'Nothing personal. It's just that Orac could have sent for help. You couldn't.'

'Nobody's perfect. What about the ship Servalan left?'

'That's a bit dented too,' Dayna said.

Vila clenched his fists and pounded his knees. 'And we're stuck on this miserable planet for the rest of our lives!' A snarling scream cut piercingly through the night air. Vila hurriedly piled more logs on the fire. 'Not that that's likely to be very long.'

Avon stood up and dusted himself off. Cally was dead but life had to go on. 'First light tomorrow we'll make for the high ground to the south.'

'Is it worth the effort?' Tarrant asked sceptically.

'Are you ready to lay down and die?'

Tarrant pushed his hand through his curly hair, feeling his scalp gingerly. 'I think I already have.'

Vila stared morosely into the flames. '*Liberator* gone, Cally dead, no way off this armpit of a planet. He may have the right idea.'

'Well, you must please yourselves, of course,' Avon said with a politeness bordering on indifference. 'But tomorrow morning I head south, and I'm taking the gun with me.'

The scream came again, shockingly loud, much nearer.

Vila huddled closer to the fire. 'You just talked me into it.'

An hour after first light they were on the move. The bleak terrain offered no shade, and already the heat of the rising sun made walking prickly and uncomfortable. Leading the way, the gun cradled in his arm, Avon paused on a small stony hillock to survey the way ahead. He glanced over his shoulder and his mouth tightened in irritation. 'Where's Tarrant?'

Dayna dumped Orac on the ground, breathing hard, and looked behind at Vila, who also turned. Tarrant was missing.

Vila was mystified. 'He was right behind us.'

'You were supposed to be keeping an eye on him,' Dayna said testily.

'I saved his life once,' Vila protested. 'Am I supposed to make a career out of it?'

Avon was already moving back the way they had come. The wrinkled folds of scrub dusted with snow stretched endlessly away, shimmering in the heat. He said, 'You two stay here.'

'You wouldn't like to, er, leave the gun?' asked Vila.

'That's right. I wouldn't,' Avon said without stopping.

'I'll come with you then, shall I?' Vila called.

But Avon had gone, not bothering to reply. Vila squatted down on his haunches and mopped his neck. He was about to start his morning tirade of gripes and grievances when he was distracted by Dayna, who seemed to have plans of her own. He stood up. 'Where are you going?'

'I want to see what's up ahead.'

'Avon said to stay here.'

'So stay here,' Dayna's voice floated back to him as she disappeared over the next ridge.

Vila stayed, but under protest. He was edgy to begin with, and being left alone on a hostile planet wasn't his idea of fun and relaxation. Uneasily he recalled Dayna's story of the slimy green creature that had nearly gobbled her whole, and he hopped from one foot to the other in a little nervous dance. *Where was she?*

'Dayna?'

His own voice sounded thin and curiously flat, and it didn't comfort him. He crept forward a few paces, craning his neck to see over the ridge. 'Dayna?' he called more loudly. Panic began to creep up from the pit of his stomach.

'Vila——'

He almost leapt out of his skin. Dayna's voice, tense, slightly breathless.

'Give me a hand. Quickly!'

'Where are you?'

'Over here. Come *on*.'

Vila charged over the ridge, wishing he had a weapon of some kind. Any kind. He was confronted by a large bush with strange leathery leaves and took a flying leap through it, only to discover that there was nowhere to land on the other side. Instead he was falling, arms cycling the empty air. He glimpsed a steep fissure with a dark cave-like hole at the bottom. Desperately he flung out an arm, his fingernails gouging the bank, and a moment later his arm was nearly jerked out of its socket as his hand grabbed a tangle of roots and he hit the side of the precipice with enough force to stunt his growth.

Then he could do nothing except hang on while he experimented to see if his lungs were still working.

'That's a big help, Vila.' Dayna was clinging to the same tangle of roots, a couple of feet to his left. 'Thanks a lot.'

Vila grinned weakly and tried to shrug, which was impossible. From below there came a dry rattling sound, like sticks being rubbed and clicked together, followed by a low-pitched buzzing.

'What's that?' Vila gulped.

'The owner of this trap. And it's anxious to make our acquaintance.'

'What do you mean, t-trap?' With difficulty he screwed his

neck round to look over his shoulder and found himself gazing down into the hole from which were emerging two of the largest snakes he'd ever seen, or was likely to see, in his life. They were big enough to be man-eaters, and probably were, given his luck.

One of them began to glide up the side of the fissure. Its eyes were like ovals of black jet polished to a mirror finish, and in them, twice over, Vila could see Dayna and himself clinging precariously just below the lip of the bank.

'Stop it, Vila!' Dayna yelled as his efforts to scramble frantically upwards only succeeded in tearing some of the roots out of the dry soil. She kicked out at him. 'Be still! You'll have us both down there any second.'

Vila stilled, but found his voice.

'Help! Help! This is all your fault, Dayna. Help! Help! Don't just hang there, *do* something!'

'I'm open to suggestions,' the girl answered, blinking the sweat out of her eyes.

'That's what I like to hear,' said a lazily cheerful voice from above.

They looked up to find a handsome, scruffily-dressed stranger grinning down at them, his teeth vividly white against his tanned skin. Handsome or scruffy, Vila had never held their appearance against anybody.

'Get us out of here,' he wailed.

'Hurry, please,' Dayna begged, casting a glance downwards to where the snake was making excellent progress.

'Relax,' said the stranger, his grin vanishing as he clipped a fresh magazine into his handgun. 'Your problems are over.'

He pointed the muzzle of the handgun down at them and fired twice.

Half a mile away Avon raised his head at the sound of the gunfire. Squatting beside Tarrant, he said urgently, 'Can you walk?'

Tarrant passed the water bottle back and wiped his lips. 'Under the circumstances I think I can even manage to run.'

Avon hauled him roughly to his feet. 'Pass out again and I'll leave you, Tarrant. That's a promise.'

'I'm surprised you came back this time.'

'We stand a better chance as a group.' Avon scooped up the weapon. 'You said you could run. Let's do it!'

When the smoke had cleared a pair of strong, capable hands reached down and Dayna was lifted over the lip of the fissure, seemingly without effort. Together they got a grip on a white-faced Vila and pulled him clear.

The black-haired stranger peered over the edge, and just to make sure fired another burst into the snakes' nest. There was a frenzied clicking accompanied by a dry rasping croak which faded into silence.

'Never did like snakes,' the stranger remarked with a rakish grin. He was about to put the handgun in its holster when Tarrant appeared over the ridge. The stranger swung round, gun levelled. He relaxed slightly but kept his finger on the trigger.

Tarrant looked keenly at Dayna and Vila, who were both slumped on the ground, recovering from their ordeal. 'You all right?'

They nodded, and the stranger inquired pleasantly, 'How many more of you are there?'

'Just one,' said Avon, directly behind him.

The stranger started to turn. 'Stand still! Drop the gun,' Avon commanded. 'Now, move away from it. Slowly.'

The stranger did so. His movements were casual, unhurried. He watched Tarrant retrieve the gun, a kind of lazy secret smile on his lips, and then turned at last to face Avon.

'Name's Dorian. And in case you failed to notice it, I just saved the lives of your two friends here.'

Avon's own smile was sharp enough to cut diamond. 'You know what they say. No good deed goes unpunished.'

* * *

Chapter Three

Dorian stepped through the open airlock and went down the gantry steps to the flight deck. Three paces behind, Avon covered him with the high-velocity weapon, watching him like a hawk. Behind them, Vila struggled in carrying Orac, which he deposited with a grunt of relief on a contoured crash-couch. He wiped his brow and looked round glumly.

He didn't reckon much to the ship. An obsolete class of cargo freighter by the look of it, and judging by the fixtures and fittings long overdue for the breaker's yard. But if – what was the name he'd seen on the peeling hull? *Scorpio*? – if *Scorpio* had brought Dorian to the planet, presumably she could lift them off it. Yesterday wouldn't be too soon for him.

'See?' Dorian spread his arms wide. 'I told you I was alone. Now, will you stop pointing that gun at me? It's beginning to make my teeth itch.'

Avon wasn't so trusting. He glanced swiftly round the small cramped flight deck, then nodded to Vila, indicating that he should carry out a recce. 'What are you doing on this planet?' he asked the smiling Dorian.

'I could ask you the same question.'

'You could, but I have the gun.'

'I'm a salvage operator.'

'Who do you work for?'

Again the lazy smile. 'There's no profit in working for anybody except yourself.'

Vila called out, 'It all looks standard enough. Except for that.'

Avon looked to where he was pointing: a small enclosed area in the prow of the vessel. If it wasn't a teleport bay, it looked remarkably like one.

He raised his eyebrows questioningly at Dorian, who shrugged nonchalantly and said. 'You tell me. I bought the ship secondhand. That was part of the standard equipment. I've never been able to figure out what the hell it was for.'

Vila's face wore a contorted expression, which meant he was thinking. 'You know what it looks like, Avon.'

'Shut up, Vila.'

Dorian stroked his darkened jaw. 'Avon and Vila . . .'

'You've heard of us?' Avon snapped.

'Should I have done? Are you in the salvage game too?'

'Yes, that's right,' Vila said, straight-faced.

'Odd,' Dorian murmured. 'I thought I knew most of the independents working in this sector.'

A pressure hatch slid open and Tarrant and Dayna entered from *Scorpio*'s rear section. 'Cargo holds and drive unit area are clear,' Tarrant reported. 'There's no one on the ship except us.'

Dayna added, 'And I've sealed the main hatches, so if there is anyone else outside that's where they're going to stay.'

'Good.' Avon permitted himself to relax. 'Any reason why we shouldn't take off?' he asked the ship's captain.

'I've come a long way to go back empty,' Dorian objected.

'What did you expect to find?' Tarrant asked him.

'The same as you, friend.'

Dayna looked puzzled. 'What was that?'

Dorian folded his arms and sighed, clearly exasperated. For the first time his casual, devil-may-care attitude showed signs of wearing thin. He said, 'Look, saving your necks was obviously a dumb thing to do, but I'm not basically stupid, right? I do know my business. And I know this is Terminal, an artificially modified planet. I also know that somewhere under the surface there's a load of valuable gear waiting to be stripped out——'

'Not any more,' Dayna interrupted.

Dorian's dark brows came together, a hatchwork of fine lines at the outer corners of his eyes. 'You mean you've already got it?'

Avon turned impatiently to Tarrant. This was irrelevant and of no importance. What mattered was getting off this planet. He wanted to move.

'Can you fly this ship?'

Tarrant surveyed the somewhat antiquated flight control modules on the semi-circular dais. Two-man operation with a rear-facing seat for the navigation officer. He nodded slowly. 'It's just a Wanderer Class planet-hopper. Mark II I'd say. Way out of date but functional.'

'I want it flown, not catalogued. Well?'

Tarrant stepped up and dropped into the pilot's seat. 'No problem,' he said, flicking switches.

'One problem.' Dorian took a menacing half-step forward. 'It happens to be my ship.'

Avon swung the gun up until the snub-nosed muzzle was staring him in the face. 'No problem,' he said placidly.

Dorian's fists clenched at his sides, and then his shoulders slumped. He turned away so that Avon couldn't see the sly glint of amusement in his eyes and sprawled out on one of the crash-couches below the gantry rail.

Businesslike, Tarrant was acclimatising himself to the *Scorpio*'s control systems. It was a bit like piloting a basic training simulator, and in fact reminded him of his early days as a rookie at the Federation Space Academy. Aeons ago. Before he graduated as Starship Captain, Alpha Grade, and before he absconded with a Chaser Class pursuit ship. From that moment on he became a wanted man, which was why, albeit reluctantly, he'd thrown in his lot with this motley crew. Still, even Avon's company was better than spending the rest of his natural life in a Federation Penal Colony on the rim of the unexplored galaxies. Though only just.

He activated the pressure sealing system and the hatches leading to the rest of the ship slid shut with soft pneumatic sighs.

'It's okay,' Vila reassured an apprehensive Dayna. 'On these old cargo ships only the main flight desk is pressurised.'

'That'll be cosy,' she said, none too impressed by the

somewhat limited quarters. But after the vastness of the *Liberator* any ship would seem claustrophobic, she supposed.

Vila sidled up and circled her slim waist with his arm. 'Would you rather be snuggling up to those snakes?' he murmured into her ear.

Dayna removed the offending arm. 'Can I think about it and let you know?'

Without looking up from the instrument console, Tarrant asked Dorian if there was anything special to watch out for; he was wary of these old cargo tubs. They had tantrums.

Dorian gave him a crooked grin. 'You want me to help you hi-jack my own ship?'

'If I get it wrong you'll be as dead as the rest of us.'

'You're the pilot, you work it out.' Dorian clasped his hands behind his head and stretched out. 'I don't give much for my chances either way,' he said, looking at Avon.

'What was that?' Vila asked in alarm.

They'd all felt the shudder pass through the deck. Then it was gone, just as quickly.

'Tarrant?' Avon barked.

The young pilot scanned the readouts and dials, his keen eyes everywhere at once. 'Not us. Outside the ship——'

Everyone swayed and Dayna had to grab hold of the bolted-down chart table as another, more violent tremor shook the flight deck.

Dorian swung his legs down and crossed to the panel of winking lights in the forward bulkhead. 'Slave?'

'Yes, Master.'

'Analyse exterior disturbance.'

'It is an earthquake, Master.'

'Cause?' Avon asked the computer.

Silence.

'Cause?' Dorian repeated. Programmed to respond to his voice-print and no other, the computer answered: 'Further sub-surface explosions of great depth and power. Magnitudes and positions are as follows: northern meridian 23 degrees——'

'Skip that! What do we expect to happen next?'

'My poor abilities do not allow expectations, Master. Readings indicate, however, an imminent earthquake followed by severe volcanic activity in this entire region.'

Dorian strode across the flight deck. 'It'll be safer and quicker if I take her up.'

Barely had he uttered the words when the deck canted steeply. The whole ship creaked with the strain and several loose items of equipment skittered across the floor. Avon grabbed the gantry rail while Vila and Dayna hung on to the bolted chart table. Dorian, caught in mid-stride, wasn't so lucky. He made a vain despairing lunge and then fell heavily, the sound of his head cracking against the gantry steps making Vila wince.

Deep, deep down, as if from the bowels of the planet, came an ominous rumbling.

Avon was already moving. Every second was vital now. Strapping himself into the co-pilot's seat alongside Tarrant, he rapped out orders to Dayna and Vila. 'Make him secure——' jerking his head at the unconscious Dorian '—— and then strap yourselves in ready for take-off. Come on, Tarrant, let's see how good you really are.'

Now, when it mattered, the two men worked as a smooth, efficient team. They'd been through a lot together. It wasn't going to end here, on this stinking planet.

'Main gyros.'

'Check, clear.'

'Drives one and two.'

'Check, green.'

'Orbital booster.'

'Check, primed.'

The tremors were every few seconds now, fiercer each time, the ship trembling and creaking in every seam. All it needed was for the ground to give way under one of the stabiliser support pads and it would be farewell and amen. Swallowed by a gigantic crack . . . to be swiftly followed by a molten lava bath and a gentle squeeze from ten million tons of fluid magma.

Dorian was now strapped in and Dayna and Vila were fastening buckles on their own crash-couches. Checks completed, Tarrant announced:

'All flight systems are green and set for go.' He took a breath and stabbed a square red button. Another kind of shudder took possession of the ship as the main drive units fired and started to build. The pulsing whine mounted until Tarrant had to raise his voice. 'Count is two minutes and running. Better strap down tight, everyone. I haven't lifted one of these into orbit too often.'

Flat down, Dayna said, 'How often?'

'Once.'

Vila raised his head, round-eyed, sweat gleaming on his neck. 'When was that?' he croaked.

'In about one minute and forty-five seconds,' Tarrant replied, concentrating on his visual readouts.

Avon's comment was blunt and not altogether ironic. 'If we last that long.'

All eyes were glued on the central digital display, silently, agonisingly slowly, marking off the seconds. The rumbling from deep below ground was louder than the high-pitched whine of the engines. Each shuddering tremor threatened to topple them over.

But it was taking too long – too long – and Vila's nerve were stretched almost to snapping point. They snapped.

'Get this thing off the ground, Tarrant!' he screamed.

'Ten seconds,' said Tarrant, his voice firm and steady. 'Five. Four——'

'Main drives running true,' Avon said calmly.

As the digital display touched zero Tarrant wrapped his hands round the twin control columns, the two finger-groved grips extensions of the arm-rests. He eased back with a steady, unrelenting pressure.

'All drives on,' he said aloud. And under his breath, '*Lift, you scruffy bag of bolts. Lift!*'

The ship heaved, fighting itself free of the exploding planet's tremendous gravitational pull. The roar of the

27

straining drive units drowned out everything else in an ocean of ear-splitting sound. Rising slowly upwards on her vertical thrusters, *Scorpio* left behind the churning mass of volcanic activity breaking through the planet's crust like a crazed pattern of veins on an aged crumbling face.

Tarrant reached out and thumbed a control switch. In the next instant he was flung back into his seat as the ship's main boosters thrust them with numbing force through the atmosphere and into deep space.

For once Vila kept his complaints to himself. Difficult to do otherwise with his mouth smeared back to his earlobes.

Tarrant unwrapped his tingling hands from the control columns and arched his neck to unlock the cramped muscles. That had been one for the record tapes.

'Primary orbit achieved,' he said, feeling quite pleased with himself. He grinned across at Avon. 'As I said. No problem.'

But Avon had his eyes fixed on the central display on which sequences of digital data were rapidly building up, line by line. At the same time everyone felt the trajectory of the ship change. Then came the rising hum of the main drive units, which zoomed up beyond audible range.

'What's going on?' Dayna said, sliding off the crash-couch.

Avon watched the large screen, unblinking. 'We are.'

'What have you done, Tarrant?' Vila asked, fumbling to release his straps. 'I didn't save your life so you could keep risking mine.'

Avon said, 'Dorian's pre-programmed his flight computer.'

'To do what?'

'Take him home, presumably,' Tarrant answered, trying to make sense of the solid block of data. Impossible without knowing the astro-navigational co-ordinates.

'To where his friends will be waiting,' Dayna said. 'Presumably.'

Vila made a face. 'And any friend of Dorian's is unlikely to be a friend of ours.' He looked sourly at Avon. 'Given the way you pushed him around.'

'Can you override the programme?' Dayna asked.

'You saw how Slave reacted,' Avon said. 'It's obviously keyed to Dorian's voice pattern.'

'There must be a way round that,' Tarrant said.

'There is,' Avon agreed. 'If you want to disrupt every system on the ship, including life-support.'

'Could Orac do it?' said Dayna hopefully.

Avon climbed out from behind the flight control module and stepped down onto the deck. 'If I had the necessary equipment to repair Orac,' he told her. 'Which I haven't.'

'So we're stuck.'

Vila was looking at the unconscious man, still strapped in. 'I think it's high time we started being very nice to Dorian.'

Never one to stand idle, Avon said, 'There are a few things we can do. Tarrant, check the flight read-outs and run through some calculations. Maybe you can work out where we're going. Dayna, see if there's an armaments locker anywhere around. Oh yes.' She turned back. 'And I want your professional opinion on this,' Avon said, tossing her Dorian's handgun. 'Vila, keep an eye on our host. Let me know when he shows signs of coming round.'

With the other members of the crew occupied, Avon went forward to inspect the teleport bay. That a rusty old tub like this should have such a sophisticated molecular beaming device intrigued him. It wasn't the only thing about this ship and her owner that didn't add up.

Dayna had located the armaments locker in the starboard bulkhead. She called Vila across, requiring his expert locksmith's skills to open it. Anything Vila couldn't open hadn't been invented. He rubbed his fingertips together while he studied it. Palm-print locking mechanism. He'd cut his teeth on these.

Taking a short silver probe from his belt, he ran the pointed tip along each side of the rectangular plate, then chose a particular area, pressed a button in the end of the

29

probe, and delicately laid his palm on the plate. The panel slid back, revealing a double-tiered rack of powerful-looking weaponry. There were magazine clips, ammunition belts, and boxes of high-velocity shells.

It was an impressive display; they were both impressed.

'Looks like Dorian's a gun freak,' Vila observed.

'There's nothing freaky about these.' Dayna took down one of the sleek lightweight handguns and balanced it in her palm. Her eyes gleamed. 'They're beautiful. Look at this.' She selected a magazine clip and slotted it into the weapon.

'So?'

'Each of these is a different mode,' Dayna explained, her fingers playing over the stacked magazines. 'Clip them into the basic handgun and you've got a weapon for every occasion. Laser, plasma bullet, percussion shell, micro-grenade, stun, drug, they're all here.' She hefted the weapon and gazed at it admiringly. 'I worked for nearly a year on a gun like this. Never did get it right.'

'Just goes to prove what I've always said,' Vila smirked. 'Stealing's quicker.'

Avon had completed his examination of the teleport bay and its control console. His original surmise had been correct. In principle it was all here; in practice it wasn't. Working from the right premise, the inventor had reached the wrong conclusion.

'I thought *Liberator* was the only ship with teleport,' said Tarrant, standing at his elbow.

'It was.' Avon made a dismissive gesture. 'This was just someone's unsuccessful attempt to develop something similar.'

'Dorian's?'

'Seems unlikely,' Avon said, turning away. 'Did you run the calculations?'

Tarrant nodded. 'Our destination is Xenon. Mean anything to you?'

'No.'

'Pity. Me neither.' The young pilot stroked his chin. 'I

checked it out on the charts. The planet Xenon is in a system well outside Federation territory.'

Avon glanced at him sharply. 'Before the war?'

'It was outside then, and it's well beyond Federation borders now their empire's contracted.' He eyed Avon shrewdly. 'You could even say it was safe – if we knew what the hell was waiting for us there. The computer won't give me any data worth a damn.'

'I didn't think it would.'

They stood before the panel of winking lights and Tarrant said, 'Isn't this rather a sophisticated piece of equipment for a salvage hauler?'

'It's very sophisticated by any standard. Someone spent a lot of time modifying a basic machine.'

'Someone else spent a lot of time developing these,' said Dayna, showing them the handguns. 'They're the best I've ever seen.'

Avon looked at the figure on the crash-couch. He said thoughtfully, 'It's beginning to look as though Dorian's got a lot of very bright associates.'

'And we've got a lot of trouble,' said Vila gloomily.

Dayna gave him a dazzling smile. 'Cheer up, Vila. You've got a lot of very bright associates too.'

'Oh yeah?' He stuck his tongue in his cheek. 'Name six.'

Chapter Four

Lit by bright, glareless ceiling panels, the underground control room was clinically clean, quiet, and empty. Banks of luminous green dials and gauges in stainless steel casings lined the walls. There was a large screen, at the moment blank, above a communications console with silver-stemmed microphones and slider controls.

Electronic relays chattered discreetly. A moving dot traced a mountain peak on a gridded screen. Other instruments ticked to themselves and exchanged messages in their own binary language.

Suddenly a shrill, penetrating alarm beeped insistently, drowning the peaceful electronic murmuring.

Footsteps clattered on metal stairs. A door slid open and a young girl entered. She was in her early twenties, blonde, and very lovely; the shiny one-piece coverall she was wearing shimmered with reflected highlights, emphasising her beautifully-proportioned figure. A belt and holstered handgun was slung low on her slender hips.

She crossed to the main instrument panel and killed the alarm. Studying an angled screen on which a blue dot glowed in a bullseye of concentric circles, the girl flicked a row of actuators and scanned the readouts. Her full-lipped mouth softened in the ghost of a smile.

At the communications console she fractionally adjusted a calibrated dial and spoke into the hand mike:

'*Scorpio*, this is Xenon base, do you copy?' She listened to the hiss of static over the speaker, and said again in her low, husky voice, '*Scorpio, Scorpio*, this is base, do you copy?'

Only the crackling hiss of empty space answered.

Vila gnawed at a thumbnail. 'Perhaps we should answer,' he said uncertainly, staring at the speaker grille.

'Terrific idea, Vila,' Dayna said dryly. 'Let's warn them we're coming.'

'They might be friendly.' Vila rather liked the sound of that voice, even distorted as it was over the channel.

'You want to take the chance?'

'He did save our lives,' Vila pointed out, nodding to where Dorian lay, unstrapped, with Avon standing over him.

'*Xenon base calling Scorpio. Come on, Dorian. I had to wake up, I don't see why you shouldn't.*' The voice sharpened impatiently. '*Wake up, Dorian!*'

'Do as the lady says, Dorian.' Avon pressed the muzzle of

the handgun against the exposed throat. He said gently, 'Wake up now or sleep for good. The choice is yours . . .'

The eyelids opened slowly. But the eyes were perfectly steady and clear. Dorian sighed. 'How did you know?'

'You took quite a crack, but you should have surfaced long before now.' Avon jerked the barrel, gesturing him to rise, and Dorian sat up as the distorted voice delivered its ultimatum:

'Listen, Dorian, I'm going to override that creepy flight computer of yours and leave you in orbit while I catch up on my sleep. Unless you answer me right now.'

Avon prodded him with the barrel. 'Answer her.'

But Dorian shook his head. 'You're going to kill me anyway, sooner or later.'

'You'd prefer it sooner?' Avon said, and his tone left not the slightest doubt that he was indifferent whichever way.

Dorian brushed his long black hair out of his eyes and rose wearily. He seemed older, his face lined with fatigue. He moved to the dais and leaned across the flight control module. Avon positioned himself so that the handgun was pointing squarely between his eyes. Avon nodded. Dorian thumbed a switch.

'Xenon base, Xenon base. This is *Scorpio*. Do you copy?'

'About time, Dorian. I have satellite visual confirmation.' The husky voice paused, as if the girl were checking readouts. *'Orbit and landing sequences are green. Confirm.'*

'Confirmed.' Dorian looked into Avon's hooded eyes. 'Sorry I kept you waiting, Soolin. Small problem——' his eyes flicked down to the white finger on the trigger '——with the communicator.'

'Apology accepted. Out.'

Dorian broke the connection and straightened up. 'You won't get away with this, you know.'

A staccato buzzer sounded. Tarrant moved into the pilot's position. 'We're approaching the atmosphere. Better get strapped in again.' To Dorian he said, 'Are your automatics adequate?'

'Slave can handle the landing.' A different mood seemed to have settled over Dorian. Almost a different personality. Harder, more astute. As if his casual manner and scruffy appearance were part of a carefully calculated masquerade.

Dayna found him an attractive enigma. She said, 'Why call a computer Slave?'

'A joke, I suppose.' Though he wasn't smiling any more.

'Someone has a very expensive sense of humour,' Avon remarked.

Dorian said gravely, 'Everything has a price, Avon. You have to decide whether you want to pay it or not. That's all.'

'I don't believe in paying,' Vila boasted.

Then Dorian said something that made them all turn to stare at him. This was the new Dorian speaking, not the old.

'You mean you're here by choice?' he said quietly.

The landing was noisy, the flight deck filled with the roaring whine of the drive units and the scream of the atmosphere against the hull. But compared with the take-off it was a joy-ride.

Scorpio descended on her retro-thrusters to the surface of Xenon, guided with pinpoint accuracy to a flat, featureless plain. Below her, two huge horizontal doors moved apart and she disappeared from view into the underground silo. The doors closed above her.

The crew prepared for disembarkation. Everyone was issued with a handgun and ammunition belt. Tarrant closed down the ship's systems and activated the pressure hatches. Then they were ready to face whatever awaited them.

Avon ordered Dorian to carry Orac. Dorian pointed to the transparent rectangular container which to the uninitiated looked like a hotch-potch of solid-state circuitry, thrown together rather than assembled.

'This?'

'That.' Avon gestured with the handgun. 'Now lead the way. Carefully.'

Dorian went up the gantry steps and through the airlock

with Avon at his heels. The rest followed. Bringing up the rear, Vila happened to notice Avon's discarded high-velocity weapon leaning against a locker. He picked it up, liking its heavier, more solid feel. Anyway, two guns were better than one. He holstered the handgun and slipped the snub-nosed weapon under his arm.

Once in the steel-lined corridor leading from the silo, Avon halted, waiting for everyone to assemble. Vila was the last to arrive. Behind him, a three-inch thick reinforced steel door slid shut with a sound like the closing of a tomb. 'Avon! This is a security door.'

Avon jabbed the handgun into Dorian's back. 'How's it opened?'

'It isn't. Unless I choose to open it.'

'Stand still!' Avon rapped as Dorian began to move.

Dorian stopped but didn't turn. 'If you kill me you'll never get back into that silo,' he said mildly. 'And that ship is the only way off this planet.'

'Terrific,' was Vila's comment. 'We're marooned again.'

'Avon's quite capable of killing you, you know,' Tarrant told Dorian.

'I never doubted it,' Dorian replied, unperturbed.

Dayna said, 'Beneath that cold exterior beats a heart of pure stone.'

Dorian half-turned his head. 'Shall we go?'

Avon lowered his handgun. 'Why not?' he said.

The transformation in Dorian fascinated him. The man seemed completely unconcerned for his own safety, as if physical threats had no relevance. And there was something else. Something even more disturbing. When he'd first set eyes on Dorian, Avon had reckoned him to be in his mid-thirties. Yet now, following close behind along the steel-lined corridors, Avon could see streaks of grey in the long black hair that he could have sworn weren't there before. Even his voice was different. Definitely that of an older man. It was weird and unsettling.

Just as unsettling was the reception awaiting them.

The room was quite large, dimly lit, tastefully furnished, with hanging curtains of greenery. In one corner, a bar glittered with bottles and glasses. On a large round table in the centre of the room had been set a crystal decanter of wine and seven glasses. The delicately perfumed air immediately brought to mind an opulent oasis of peace and calm amidst a barren, inhospitable environment. Everything had been selected with great care and not a little expense. It was a rich man's refuge.

From out of the shadows appeared a girl. She was stunningly beautiful. The one-piece coverall clung to her like a shiny second skin. Avon stared, unable to tear his eyes away.

Dorian placed Orac on the deep-pile carpet and went to greet her. He kissed her lightly on the cheek, as a father might kiss his daughter, and a slight frown disturbed her flawless face.

'Are you all right?'

Dorian smiled wanly. 'A little tired. It took longer than I expected.'

He looked more than tired, Avon thought. Exhausted. Face heavily lined and deathly pale. The streaks of grey showed prominently, even in the subdued light. *What was happening to the man?*

Dorian turned, holding out his hand. 'May I present Soolin. My companion.'

Avon moved further into the room, his eyes probing the shadows. 'Where are the others?'

It was Soolin's low, husky voice which answered. 'There are no others.'

She poured wine into one of the crystal glasses and gracefully offered it to him. Avon didn't move. Her lips curved in a smile and she sipped from the glass herself.

Then she poured another glass of wine and handed it to Dorian, who held it up to the light and drank. 'I wouldn't poison a good wine, Avon. If I wanted you dead there are much more direct ways to achieve it. I could snap my fingers——'

He snapped them and Soolin's gun was aimed unwaveringly at Avon's chest. The speed of the draw caught them all unprepared. Even Dayna, no mean markswoman herself, was impressed.

'——And you're dead,' said Dorian. He nodded. Soolin twirled the handgun and holstered it. 'Fast, isn't she? Now, Soolin, be so good as to pour my guests some wine.' He regarded the four watchful faces with a hint of amusement in his eyes. 'Surely now you can bring yourselves to trust me?'

'He who trusts can never be betrayed,' Avon murmured. 'Only mistaken. Cally once told me that was a saying among her people.'

'Cally?'

'She was murdered. So were most of her people.'

Tarrant said, 'Seven glasses.'

Soolin raised her head from pouring the wine. She arched an eyebrow. 'I'm sorry?'

'You laid out one glass too many.'

Vila bustled forward, tossing the snub-nosed weapon aside, heedless of where it landed behind a chair, rubbing his hands briskly. 'Not to worry. I'll drink the extra one.' He grabbed a glass and drank, smacking his lips appreciatively.

'If you'll excuse me.' Dorian finished his wine and placed the glass on the table. 'I have things to attend to. When you're ready, Soolin will show you to your quarters. You'll find everything you need there, including fresh clothes. We'll talk again when you're rested.' He spread his arms and his tired face relaxed into a smile full of warmth and charm. 'You really are most welcome here, my friends.'

When he had gone Tarrant moved to Avon's side. Keeping his voice low so that Soolin shouldn't overhear, he said, 'What do you think?'

Avon pursed his lower lip between thumb and finger. 'I think his taste in wine, and women, is impeccable,' he said.

Tarrant's eyes clouded. 'Why do I get the feeling he's been in complete control of everything we've done right from the beginning?'

'Because you're not as stupid as you look, Tarrant. None of us are. With one possible exception.' He swivelled on one heel and Tarrant followed his gaze to where Vila was eagerly proffering his glass for a refill.

They heard Soolin say, with a smile, 'I see you're a connoisseur.'

Vila smirked modestly. 'I appreciate the best, whenever I can get it.' Brow furrowed, he leaned towards the young, shapely blonde girl. 'Tell me, Soolin. What exactly does a . . .' he cleared his throat '. . . companion do?'

Coolly, Soolin said, 'Nothing you could cope with.'

'Ah.' Vila scratched behind his ear and smiled glassily.

Standing by his shoulder, Dayna said impishly, 'Next question.'

'Can I help it if I've got a weakness for lady gunfighters?' said Vila sorrowfully, watching Soolin's slender figure moving to the door.

'You've got a weakness for ladies of any description.'

'I'm just naturally affectionate,' Vila protested.

'If you'd like to follow me,' Soolin said, standing by the open door.

There was a momentary hesitation until Avon led the way. He had a lot on his mind. Too much to spare a thought for Orac.

Chapter Five

The chamber was hollowed out of solid seamless rock. Walls, floor and ceiling emitted the very faintest of blue phosphorescent glows, which was smothered by the dense blackness. From somewhere came the distant, echoing reverberation of dripping water, a sound that seemed to intensify the silence and deepen the gloom. Time was suspended here, held in abeyance.

If anything lived in this subterranean pit, where the air was dank and foul, it was not human.

There was the hollow, grating sound of a heavy stone trap-door. A pale shaft of light filtered from above, dimly illuminating a circular iron stairway. The careful tread of descending footsteps, the soft scuffling scrape of leather against slimy, corroding metal.

Dorian crouched at the bottom of the stairway, one hand on the rail, staring blindly into the darkness. His face had aged terribly. His hair was now almost totally grey. What a short time ago had been a lean, strong body was now bent and frail.

Reluctantly, fearfully, he let go of the rail and advanced a few faltering steps. The pinched, shrunken mouth parted as he sucked in the chill air. His breath rasped in his throat.

'Are you there . . .?'

He took another step into the enveloping, palpable darkness. Then, hoarsely: 'I have them . . . they are here.'

Something was approaching. It moved with infinite slowness, dragging itself forward, hauling itself with such tremendous effort that its breathing was ragged and laboured. It came on, heaving itself nearer, its breathing booming louder and louder until it was almost upon him and Dorian cried, 'Enough! Close enough!'

He wouldn't look directly at it, and when he spoke it was inwardly, as if to himself. The presence, unseen, waited behind the veil of darkness, near enough for him to have heard its heartbeat had it possessed one.

'One of them was killed before I got there. But the group remains . . . bound together by time and pain and the need to survive. The death of the telepath Cally will make it more difficult. But they can still be used.'

(SOON!)

The sound was everywhere, in the rock, inside his skull, but it hadn't come from a living throat.

(IT MUST BE SOON!)

The faint blue phosphorescence of the chamber suddenly

blazed with vivid blinding intensity. It transferred itself to Dorian so that he was surrounded by a crackling, glowing ball of energy.

His eyes became slits of pain and his face opened in a scream of agony. For a moment his spine was jerked straight, galvanised to his full height on a rack of brilliant blue lightning, and then as it ebbed away he slumped to his knees, sobbing, moaning, until he passed mercifully into unconsciousness.

But the sobbing and moaning didn't cease. Muted now, they came from the presence in the darkness, which had no throat to utter them.

The door slid open and Avon flitted like a shadow into the darkened room. His feet made no sound on the thick pile carpet as he moved towards the nearest sculptured armchair. By the room's single subdued light, masked by broad fronds of vegetation like wilting green hands, he saw that the decanter and glasses had been cleared away. And something else had been removed.

Orac.

A muscle rippled in his cheek as he silently cursed himself for a fool. They had accepted Dorian's hospitality, the new clothing, even armed themselves with his weapons. They had drunk wine with him and his beautiful, mysterious 'companion'. And like idiots (no, he was the idiot, he blamed himself and no one else) had forgotten the one vital, all-important thing that might save them from destruction.

Avon stood in the centre of the luxurious, darkened room, fists bunched by his sides, Dorian's words floating back to mock him . . .

Everything has a price, Avon. You have to decide whether you want to pay it or not. That's all.

Supple and dextrous, the fingers manipulated the short silver probe underneath the base of the raised locking mechanism. The mechanism was contained in a small square box about two-thirds of the way down the extra-heavy-duty reinforced door. And – nasty thought – it could be lead-lined, which would effectively block the probe's low frequency pulses.

'Get on with it, Vila!' fumed Tarrant. He spoke over his shoulder, while his eyes kept watch on the steel-walled corridor.

'Will-you-keep-your-voice-down,' Vila said in a martyred whisper.

As a straightforward girl, all that Dayna required was a straight answer. 'Can you get it open or not?'

'*Not*,' Vila hissed irritably. 'I told Avon that. Didn't I say there was no point in trying?'

Tarrant: 'You always say there's no point in trying.'

Dayna: 'But you usually manage to come up with something.'

'Not this time!' Vila checked his annoyance. He decided to be very calm and very patient. 'Not without a lot of equipment, peace and quiet and co-operation. And in case you haven't noticed, the lady with the gun is not basically a co-operative person. I don't think she'd be all that happy about us trying to borrow her boyfriend's ship. Especially without his permission.'

Dayna nodded towards an adjacent corridor, at right-angles to the one they were in. 'Maybe there's another entrance to the silo.'

'Worth a look,' Tarrant agreed.

'No, it isn't,' Vila snapped as the pair started to move away. Then remembered he was being calm and patient, and went on in an even, reasonable tone. 'If there is another entrance it'll have the same security system as this.'

'You're probably right,' Tarrant said at the corner. He flashed a bright smile. 'So you stay here and keep working on that.'

'What!'

'We'll let you know if we find an easier one,' Dayna promised him.

Vila sighed and straightened up. 'What about Avon?'

'Tell him where we've gone,' said Tarrant.

'He won't like it.'

Tarrant bit his lip and looked distraught. Then he winked. 'Pity about that,' he said, and was gone.

Vila glared after him and bent once more, the silver probe balanced delicately in his finger tips. But there he paused, his mouth set stubbornly.

'No,' he said, addressing the locking mechanism. 'Why should I? I don't have to justify my existence by going through the motions of trying to open a door that I know is impossible. I'm the expert. If I say it's impossible, it's impossible.' He nodded once, quite convinced by the argument, stood up straight and slipped the probe into his belt.

'To hell with it. I wonder where they keep that wine.'

'I naturally took the opportunity to study all the systems of the *Liberator*. A few – a very few – were of minor interest. I would not, however, number the teleport system amongst these.'

Orac sat on a bench in the Operations Room lit glarelessly by the overhead panels, while he delivered himself of his opinion. His tone was brisk and rather dismissive. Such trifles were beneath his superior intellect. He resented having to waste time which could be much better spent on loftier, more abstruse matters. Whether the universe was cyclic, entropic, or open-ended, for instance.

'Nevertheless, you do know how it worked,' said Dorian. He stood with arms folded, feet apart, studying this magic box of electronic wizardry with an intense, almost fervid expression on his smooth tanned face. His long black hair was swept back in a glossy wave. Rings glittered on his fingers. His immaculate dark blue tunic was richly embroidered at collar and cuffs with motifs of gold and scarlet.

'Of course I know how it worked,' replied Orac waspishly. Never one to suffer fools, his tolerance threshold was exceedingly low.

'Then you'll tell me. Now.'

'There seems little point in wasting time on such an explanation since you would be incapable of understanding it.'

Dorian raised his chin a fraction. 'Don't be insolent.'

'A statement of fact cannot be insolent,' Orac informed him blandly. 'Besides, insolence implies an emotional relationship which does not, and could not, exist between us.'

From the doorway Avon said, 'Orac must make a refreshing change from that flight computer of yours.'

Without turning, Dorian said quietly, 'Come on in, Avon.'

Avon strolled across, his practised eye noting the gleaming banks of equipment, the large scanner screen, the deep space detector display. This was a comprehensive and highly advanced command control and communications centre. He tapped Orac lightly with his finger. 'Neat job.'

'Thank you.' Dorian accepted the compliment without false modesty.

'I thought you'd probably have the necessary repair facilities somewhere around, but I didn't expect you to do the work as well.'

'Who designed it?' asked Dorian abruptly.

'His name was Ensor.'

'I should have known.' Dorian nodded and smiled to himself. 'He was never a gracious man. Orac reflects his personality.'

'Orac was the culmination of his life's work.' Avon removed the activator key and Orac's circuitry faded. 'Ensor bequeathed it to an associate of mine. Who bequeathed it to me.' He slipped the activator into his pocket and zipped it shut. Then he leaned casually against the bench and looked at Dorian. 'You must have been very young when you met Ensor.

'Must I?'

'He spent the last twenty years of his life in hiding.'

'Then I must have been very young.'

'Did you carry out the modifications on that flight computer?'

'Yes.' Dorian's handsome face was impassive. 'I created Slave.'

Avon gripped the holstered handgun at his hip. 'And these?'

'Those as well.'

'And what about——' Avon let his eyes roam round the room '——all this?'

'I found the tunnels and chambers already here. I merely had them adapted to my particular needs.'

Avon folded his arms and the two men stared at one another.

'What did you do in your spare time?'

Tarrant led the way down the winding metal stairway with Dayna a few steps behind. Their feet clanged hollowly and the sound bounced back from the stone walls of the brightly-lit stairwell. Descending to the next level, Tarrant paused and leaned over the rail, peering downwards. He was short of breath. Still not fully recovered, he realised. The flight from Terminal had taken a lot out of him.

'Don't tell me you're tired already,' Dayna tutted unsympathetically.

Tarrant glanced up at her lithe form, even more pantherish than usual in a zippered black leather suit that was moulded to her athletic body. He scowled and gestured wearily. 'Look, we must be at least four levels below the landing silo——'

'At least.'

'——so wherever this leads, it isn't to an underfloor access tunnel.'

'Probably not,' Dayna agreed chirpily. 'But aren't you curious to find out where it *does* lead?'

'In a word, no.'

'Well, I am.'

Tarrant sighed and closed his eyes. 'I was afraid of that.'

'You stay here, then, and I'll carry on.'

Stung, Tarrant replied tartly, 'Listen, you'll be old yourself one day. Then you'll be sorry.' Reluctantly, he started on down.

Behind him, Dayna said, 'I don't know what you're moaning about. Vila's probably got the door open by now.'

'There's an irritating thought,' Tarrant muttered.

'I knew you'd like it,' she said with a grin.

Finally they reached the lowest level, which was a distinct disappointment. The bottom of the circular stairway ended in a short corridor, sealed off at either end. There were no doors, no signs of further access at all.

'Dead end,' Tarrant pronounced smugly.

'It can't be,' Dayna said, standing with hand on hips. She slowly revolved to look both ways. 'I mean, why bother with all those stairs?'

'Good point. I seem to remember making it on the way down.'

'I hate people who say I told you so.'

'So do I.' Tarrant put his foot on the bottom step. 'But sometimes it's irresistible.'

'There has to be *something* here,' Dayna insisted, running her hands along the blank walls and gazing up at the ceiling.

'Come on, let's go back. If Avon gets to that ship and we're not there I wouldn't put it past him to leave without us.'

Dayna was still searching. She didn't like unsolved mysteries. She said absently, 'He needs you to fly it.'

'Only if Slave won't accept his orders.'

'Which it won't.'

'It will if Orac's working,' Tarrant said. This was wasting time, besides being pointless. He went up a few more steps and then hung back for a moment. 'Come on, Dayna. We can be of more use up there than down here.'

He was right, of course, Dayna thought, as Tarrant disappeared up the winding stairway. Still, it irked her not to know the purpose of this short stretch of empty passageway deep underground. She gave it one last puzzled look and turned back to mount the stairway. Then stopped dead, her hand on the rail, at the sound of a heavy stone trap-door.

Spinning round, she saw a black oblong opening in the floor of the corridor. Inside she glimpsed steps leading down.

'I knew it!' Dayna told herself triumphantly. 'Tarrant!' she shouted up the stairwell, before hurrying to kneel by the opening. The bottom of the iron stairway was swallowed up in inky darkness.

'Get a move on, Dayna,' Tarrant called distantly.

Cupping her hands, Dayna shouted, 'I've found it!' and stepped down into the oblong hole, cautiously feeling her way.

Tarrant's faint 'Found what?' was the last thing she heard as her head vanished below floor level, and at once a dank chill struck through to her bones and her nose wrinkled at the foul musty odour.

On the bottom step she hesitated and almost turned back, but curiosity overcame her. The light from above illuminated a small area at the base of the stairway but nothing more. Dayna squinted into the gloom.

The soles of her boots encountered something slimy, like a slug's trail. Dayna went very still, all her senses alert. Her heart began to pound violently. Cold sweat beaded her forehead. Her eyes ached with the strain of trying to discern what was lurking there in the blackness. Because she was now convinced that something was.

And then it happened so quickly she was unprepared, frozen in her tracks.

A heavy liquid dragging sound, a loud hoarse wheezing, and it was coming for her, moving with a speed she would not have thought possible. Her knees turned to water and her arms became like lead weights. Then pure terror broke through the paralysis and she whipped out the handgun, aimed it at arm's length in the direction of the loathsome sound, and squeezed the trigger.

Nothing happened. She pulled the trigger again, and nothing happened. And again – the thing was very near now, almost upon her – and again nothing happened.

It was on the very edge of the darkness. Dayna backed away, turned and leapt desperately for the stairway. She hadn't reached it when the stone trap-door began to close.

The oblong of light became a square, and then a narrower oblong, and then a slit.

'*Tarrant!*'

Her scream was muffled in the chamber, as if she was underwater.

The trap-door closed, sealing her in utter pitch darkness.

Above the hammering of her heart Dayna heard it slithering nearer, and nearer, and nearer.

'What is it, Dayna, what's wrong?'

Tarrant clattered down the winding stairway and stood poised, halfway down, and stared incomprehendingly along the empty corridor.

'Dayna——?'

He came down the last half-dozen steps in a rush and looked wildly to left and right.

'Dayna?' His voice rose. 'Dayna!'

Grimly, trying to control his panic, Tarrant began to search every square inch of the walls and floor.

Chapter Six

Dorian said, 'I was hoping you might be able to help me with it.'

'It's not really my field.'

'No?'

Avon shook his head. The teleport bay in the Operations Room was on the same crude pattern as the one in the ship. And just as impracticable, in its present state. While not an expert in molecular teleportation, he'd had sufficient experience to know that. He said, 'For what it's worth it looks to me as though you'll need to start again from scratch and try a different approach.'

'I've already tried four different approaches.'

'I meant go back to basic theoretical principles.'

Dorian watched him steadily. 'That's what I did.'

'Working alone.'

'Of course.'

Avon smiled sceptically. 'At a conservative estimate that sort of research and development would have taken you twenty years of uninterrupted effort.'

'Thirty years, actually,' Dorian corrected him.

Avon's smile evaporated. He drew his handgun, his eyes hard and flat, his mouth a thin straight line.

'All right, Dorian. Let's stop playing games.'

Dorian looked sad. He sighed gently and said, 'You disappoint me, Avon. You of all people should know that the intellect is a much more powerful weapon than the gun. Particularly when the gun doesn't work.'

Unhurriedly he drew his own handgun, watching with amused, tolerant eyes as Avon pulled the trigger of the useless weapon. Dorian shrugged and brushed a lock of black hair from his forehead. 'Soolin removed the magazine and replaced it with a dummy,' he said, almost in a tone of apology.

'While I was bathing.' Disgustedly, Avon rammed the handgun back into the holster.

Seething inside, he had no choice but to obey Dorian's command. But his face betrayed no emotion as they walked along the short connecting passage to the Crew Room with its concealed lighting and restful screens of foliage slumbering in the shadows.

Yet again, Dorian's demeanour had undergone a subtle shift, Avon noticed. As if there were several conflicting personalities inside him, battling for supremacy, each in its turn taking charge. From buccaneering salvage operator to genial host to man of science . . . and now? What next?

A touch of the conscientious host again, apparently, as Dorian invited him to sit down and offered him wine.

When Avon declined the offer, Dorian moved to the bar and poured himself a glass. He seemed momentarily disconcerted at finding several flasks of drinks already open on the bar-top. Then shrugged, dismissing it as of no consequence.

Which was rather fortunate for Vila.

Crouching out of sight at the top of the staircase, Vila breathed a long low sigh of relief and took a quick swig from the flask to steady his nerves. On hearing footsteps he'd just had time to scurry into his hiding-place. Damn lucky the room's lighting was designed for relaxation rather than illumination.

He wiped his lips, listening intently as Dorian said, 'It is necessary that you should understand what is to happen to you.'

Avon's voice was cold, unyielding. 'No it isn't. Just kill me and get it over with.'

Vila almost dropped the flask. He set it down carefully and reached for his handgun.

'In case you're expecting help,' said Dorian, 'I should warn you that your friends' guns are also useless.'

'Naturally.'

Vila turned the gun over in his hand, gazing at it dumbly.

Dorian was saying, 'Deep in the rock below this base there's a room I found when I first came here. As far as I can tell it was carved from a mineral deposit, a pocket of some element which I still know very little about. Despite nearly two hundred years of study.'

'If at first you don't succeed,' said Avon flippantly.

'You think I'm insane.'

'It had occurred to me.'

'The room exists, Avon.' Dorian's voice was very calm. 'And since I found it I haven't aged one single day. It cleanses me of all the corruptions of time and . . . appetite.'

'Appetite?'

Dorian's voice sank to a whisper. 'I can do anything, Avon. Anything.'

'Most madmen can.'

'I can indulge any taste, any sensation, any vice I wish, and the room, the room——'

'Cleanses you.'

'Exactly!'

'Dammit to hell,' Avon said matter-of-factly. 'You are insane, aren't you.'

'By now I probably would be.'

'If it wasn't for this mysterious room.'

'And what it contains.'

'And what might that be, Dorian?'

Soolin moved with catlike grace from the doorway to the centre of the room. Her hands hung by her sides, lightly flexed. Her eyes were fixed on Dorian, standing by the bar with the gun in one hand, a glass in the other.

The blonde girl said, 'You haven't answered me. What does the room contain?'

Dorian placed the glass on the bar. His mouth was smiling but his eyes weren't. He turned to face her. 'All the madness and rotting corruption which would have been mine. It contains . . . horror, Soolin.'

Avon said, 'And this horror shows itself to you, does it?'

'It will show itself,' Dorian nodded slowly, 'to all of us.'

'I think not,' Soolin murmured, watching him.

'You underestimate me, my dear.'

'The smallest movement, Dorian, is all it takes.' There was a tensity in her stance, like a spring about to be released.

'She could do it, too,' Dorian told Avon. 'Soolin was taught by the best.'

'The second-best, actually.'

'Of course, I was forgetting. You killed him, didn't you?' Dorian said to Avon, 'He was one of the men responsible for the death of her family. She killed all the others too. She's a bad enemy. But not without a gun.'

The girl's eyes narrowed fractionally.

'That's right, Soolin.'

Still watching him, she drew her handgun from the holster low on her hip. She unclipped the magazine and glanced down at it, then raised her eyes to his. 'You're right. I did underestimate you. My dear.'

Dorian gestured with the handgun. 'Move. Both of you.'

As Avon rose and followed the girl to the door, Dorian said, 'I think we'll find your friends are already waiting for us.'

When they had gone Vila's tiptoed down the staircase. he climbed slowly to his feet, looked at the redundant handgun, and tossed it aside. Then realising he had picked up the flask, he took a long pull at it. The wine left a tingling sensation on his tongue, very pleasant, though it didn't make him think any better.

In fact it was better than thinking, so he took another pull. He came round from behind the armchair, draining the last drop from the flask, and nearly sprawled full length as he stumbled over something. He dropped the flask and picked up the high-velocity weapon, which had lain there unnoticed and forgotten.

Vila checked it. It was fully loaded. He slipped the safety off and crept towards the door. The glint of bottles behind the bar caught his eye, and he paused, sorely tempted. He wiped his lips and belched softly. Then shook his head regretfully and carried on.

Drinking was better than thinking, but right now action seemed better than both.

The stone trap-door slid open and Tarrant descended the iron stairway, his eyes straining to penetrate the darkness. 'Dayna?'

Avon and Soolin came after him, and behind them, Dorian, the handgun clutched tightly in his fist. His movements were jerky and excited. He watched the three of them with a fixed, manic stare.

'Tarrant . . .'

At the sound of Dayna's voice, barely audible, Tarrant stiffened. He reached out to where she was leaning against the faintly glowing rock wall and gently took her trembling body in his arms. 'It's all right, Dayna.' He cradled her head against his chest. 'Everything's all right now.'

She clung to him, whimpering. 'There's something there . . . in the dark.'

'It's all right. You're not alone any more.'

Dorian bared his teeth in a mirthless smile. 'That's why I came for you. You care for each other. After what you've been through together you can't fail to care for each other.' He turned his head mechanically. 'Even you, Avon.'

'Spare me the amateur psychology.'

'I wouldn't expect you to admit it,' Dorian said. 'But you belong to them, just as they belong to you. And that's why I rescued you from Terminal.'

'I thought you wanted the teleport system.'

Dorian said, 'Orac will give me that. What you will give me – all of you – is *life*.'

'Killing us won't give you life,' Tarrant said, holding Dayna close.

But Dorian might not have heard. 'Soolin is a stranger to you,' he said, as if talking to the dank air, the glowing rock face. 'But one outsider can be absorbed in the gestalt.'

'Gestalt?' Soolin frowned. She glanced fearfully into the darkness.

'Together you will become one creature,' Dorian intoned. 'A gestalt. It will be a strong creature. It will absorb much more than an individual could, before it dies . . .'

Suddenly he raised his hand. Everyone was staring into the black depths of the chamber. The thing had begun to move, dragging itself with a squelchy liquid sound towards them. Its breathing swelled, hoarse and broken, magnified in the confined space. In time with its breathing the walls began to pulse with the strange blue light. As the creature neared them the light grew brighter and brighter, until the air itself seemed to crackle with a billion blue atoms of electrostatic energy.

'. . . you see? It begins. It will work. I knew it would.' Dorian's hand, held high, bunched triumphantly into a white-knuckled fist. 'The room accepts you. It will make you one and give you my death!'

Soolin shrank back behind Avon's shoulder. 'What is it?' she asked in a ghastly whisper.

'My creature will need to understand,' said Dorian, his eyes glittering with blue light. 'It must warn me of approaching death. Yours will be its understanding.'

'But what *is* it?' Soolin moaned, deeply afraid.

'That, my dear, is what you are going to replace . . . you and the others.'

'I imagine it was once a man,' Avon said, watching the formless shape materialise from the darkness. 'One of a long line who died in Dorian's place.'

'They die quickly now,' said Dorian, his pale lips drawn back. 'It has become too much for one man to bear.'

'Who was the first, Dorian?'

'My partner. We entered this place together. Like you, he could never leave it.'

'And when he started to die you found someone to replace him. And you've had to go on replacing them,' Avon said, shielding Soolin's body with his own.

Dorian laughed. 'You will last much longer than the others,' he cried gleefully.

The shape emerged like a monstrous shadow, surrounded by a blue phosphorescent glow. The light from the walls pulsed crazily, dazzling them. Avon backed away. Soolin hid her face against his shoulder. Tarrant and Dayna had retreated until their backs were against the rock face.

Through gritted teeth, Avon said, 'You're short of one man, in case you hadn't noticed.'

'Vila will join you later. Now make your goodbyes.' Dorian's face was a livid mad blue mask. 'Your lives, your consciousness, are over . . .'

Pushing Soolin to one side, Avon leapt for Dorian's throat. His hands clawed the crackling blue air, and a white hot needle lanced through the tender tissue of his brain. Avon shrieked in agony. He fell to his knees, dimly aware that everyone except Dorian had felt the same stab of pure pain.

Hands pressed to his head, Avon tried to rise, but the white hot needle glowed more fiercely, searing his brain cells. There was a voice somewhere, a voice calling his name. It was faint, yet distinct, on the outer rim of the searing white pain . . .

'Avon! Avon!'

Avon opened his eyes and saw Vila at the top of the winding stairway, the snub-nosed weapon clasped in both hands. Struggling to his feet, jaw clenched tight, Avon caught the weapon, spun round, and fired point-blank from the hip into the centre of the monstrous looming shape.

The scream and Dorian's 'No!' seemed to issue from a single throat.

Avon fired again. The shape fell, a grotesque and distorted human form, and Dorian crumpled as if he too had been shot, sinking slowly back and falling to the floor, arms spread wide. The pulsing light began to fade. And as it faded, each pulse revealed Dorian in a new light. Before their eyes he began to grow old, and with the ageing all the corruption of his life, so long hidden, began to break through.

Soolin stared as the handsome face disintegrated, the flesh wrinkling and yellowing, and had to turn away, unable to bear the final moments. She didn't see the red-crazed eyeballs turn to mushy pulp, nor the suppurating sores burst, nor the head become a scaly black ball, fissured with deep cracks.

When she looked again there was only a heap of richly-embroidered clothing spilling grey dust onto the smooth, faintly-glowing rock floor.

'Look,' Dayna said, pointing.

Where the creature had fallen, on the edge of the light from above, lay a handsome young man with a smooth tanned face and long black glossy hair.

The silence was broken by a groan. Vila sat on the top step of the stairway, clutching his head in both hands and looking queasy. 'I'm going to give up drinking,' he vowed fervently. 'It'll be pink asteroids next.'

'You know, this base could be quite useful,' Avon said, sitting back at ease in one of the armchairs. He twirled the crystal glass in his fingers, the amber highlights flickering against his thoughtful features. 'It's outside Federation territory. It's well-hidden.'

'And well-equipped,' Vila put in, leaning on the bar. He sipped the dark purple wine appreciatively. Much more mellow than the other stuff. He was getting quite a taste for it.

'Not to mention a very weird basement,' said Dayna, checking out the magazine clips she had found in the armoury.

Avon picked up the small remote control device. He looked round at the others and thumbed a button. The bottles on the shelves tinkled musically and the green foliage fluttered for a moment and then became still once more.

'Strike one basement,' he said, draining his glass. He rose to his feet and looked at Vila. 'Now, I suggest you get that landing silo open. We'll need to work on the ship.' He went towards the door. 'While I get the teleport system working.'

'Do you think you can?' Tarrant asked doubtfully.

Avon paused at the door. 'Yes. With Orac's help.'

'What about Soolin?' Dayna asked, looking up.

'She goes or stays.' Avon shrugged slightly. 'As she pleases.'

'I hope she stays,' Vila said eagerly. 'I have a thing about lady gunfighters.'

'Don't we know it,' said Dayna in a long-suffering voice.

Avon seemed reluctant to leave. There was something on his mind. He pulled an earlobe and said, 'You know, Dorian might have been telling the truth about himself and that room; but he was insane, of course. Quite insane.'

He went out, leaving behind a lingering silence in the softly-lit room.

Dayna gazed at the others. 'What brought that on?'

'Something Dorian said, I think.' Tarrant lay back on the couch, grinning into space. 'Remember? About Avon belonging to us, as we belong to him.'

'Oh well, I agree with him,' said Vila at once.
Dayna blinked. 'Dorian?'
'Avon,' said Vila, pouring more of the dark purple wine. 'Dorian was obviously insane.' He smacked his lips and drank.

PART TWO
TRAITOR

Chapter Seven

Once again the massed fleets of Federation battle cruisers swept out on missions of death and destruction to the outer planetary systems. The creed of their commanders was simple: submit to Federation rule or die.

It was a doubly bitter blow for these distant, peace-loving civilisations. Having regained their independence following the Empire's fall from power, when the Federation had retreated to lick its wounds, they were forced for the second time in galactic history to yield to a ruthless and malign authority which sought to spread its dark demon seeds amongst the stars.

Even though the odds were heavily against them, some planets put up a fierce resistance. Thus the all-mighty, all-powerful Federation – created from and dedicated to the impulse of naked aggression, a colossal war machine whose economy and industry were geared to weapons of death – found itself bogged down in a score of minor conflicts and petty skirmishes. For wherever resistance showed itself, however timidly, it had to be crushed and stamped into the ground with an iron heel.

To preserve its self-image of invincibility the Federation had to emerge the victor. And for that, there had to be a vanquished.

One such dirty little war was taking place on the planet Helotrix. Despite its cities being smashed to fragments and its countryside laid waste by the ravages of technological warfare, Helotrix and its people were being exceedingly stubborn. They ought to have given in long ago. Their struggle was futile. How could they possibly hope to win against the combined battle fleets of the Federation?

Everyone knew this, from the Federation Supreme Commander right down to the lowliest Grade IIII/P ground trooper.

Everyone, apparently, except the Helots.

The Helot sitting docilely in front of the desk was a middle-aged man with thinning grey hair and a pale, moonlike face. He was quite tall, yet his round-shouldered stooping posture made him seem only of average height. His hands, hanging limply below the tattered shirt cuffs, were soft and white.

Colonel Quute glanced up from the open file, scratching his red neck with a thick blunt forefinger. 'Igin, is that right?'

'Yes, sir,' the Helot answered placidly, staring into space.

'Attached to the fourth column of freedom fighters commanded by Star Major Hunda?'

'Yes, sir.'

Colonel Quute caught the eye of the duty tracer sitting at the plotting table. The Colonel's mouth twisted in what passed for a smile. He gave his attention to the man once more. 'Strange how you civilians give yourselves these impressive military ranks.' He leaned back, clasping his meaty hands. 'What was "Star Major" Hunda before the occupation? Hairdresser? Shoemaker?'

'No, sir. He was my first assistant at Leedenbrank,' Igin replied meekly.

'Ah, a teacher.' Colonel Quute nodded his shorn bullet head. 'You know that Leedenbrank no longer exists?'

'Yes. We heard that most of it had been destroyed.'

'Together with eighteen thousand defenders.' Quute wasn't gloating; it was merely a statistic; he was a professional. 'Though they were given the chance to surrender,' he added for the record. 'What was your position at Leedenbrank?'

'I was the director of geological studies.'

'Indeed?' Colonel Quute wormed his finger inside his ear and inspected the results. He flipped the file shut. 'All right, Igin, I'm going to let you rejoin your friends.'

The man looked confused. 'You're releasing me?'

'Of course, why not? And I think you should tell Hunda that resistance is quite pointless. We are willing to offer all rebel forces an honourable peace.' As if it didn't matter one way or the other, Colonel Quute asked, 'What was the mission you were on?'

'We wanted to find out how far the flood level below the city had receded.'

'I see. Why?'

'Hunda thought it might be possible to tunnel under the Magnetrix Terminal and lay explosive charges.'

Colonel Quute nodded slowly. 'Clever.' He massaged his broad nose. 'Yes, that would make a mess of things all right. And is the scheme feasible?'

'Not at the moment.' The older man gave the information readily, without any hint of reluctance. 'The water is still too high. We should have to tunnel over three hundred metres.'

'Well, that's something for you to report, isn't it?' said Colonel Quute jovially. 'All right, Igin. Off you go.' He waved his hand and Igin went out.

They heard him shuffling along the concrete corridor and the young duty tracer looked across at his superior, grinning. 'Too easy, isn't it, sir?'

Colonel Quute dropped the file into a tray. 'Just like children, once they've been adapted. I don't know what the stuff is the Pacification Police use, but I wish I could get hold of a shot of it.'

'Why, sir?'

'For next time I go on R and R.' Colonel Quute winked craftily. 'I'd use it to get my entertainment for nothing.' He jerked his head briskly. 'Check that he's registering.'

Studying the gridded plot screen, the duty tracer confirmed, 'Yes, we have a clear signal. He's heading out towards the refineries.'

'Good.' Colonel Quute stood up and yawned. He could use forty winks. 'Call me when you think he's made contact.'

61

He stretched his solid, thickset frame out on the bunk in the corner, and as he'd trained himself to do over twenty-three years of campaigning, fell instantly into a light dreamless sleep.

Avandir was in the sanitary cubicle. There was no ceiling, and only part of the corner wall remained standing, which gave him cover and made a convenient vantage point. Why were sanitary cubicles left partially untouched when the rest of the buildings which contained them had been blasted flat?

Interesting question. He'd write a thesis on it someday. For his doctorate. When the war was over. *If* it was ever over.

Avandir raised himself from the plastic seat and shaded his eyes. Through the dust and smoke drifting across the piles of rubble he thought he glimpsed something. A tiny figure picking its way through the desolation. The balding grey head and thin crouching body were unmistakable.

The fair-haired young man thumbed a button on his transceiver. The lines around his eyes and mouth were deeply etched, five years premature. 'Command Central, this is Surveillance Post 3. Do you read?'

The radio spat and crackled. 'Go ahead, SP3.'

'Tell Hunda that Igin is coming back.'

There was a slight pause. Then: 'Hello, SP3, this is Hunda. Is he alone?'

Avandir squinted round the broken wall. 'As far as I can see, yes.'

'All right. Hold him where he is. Tell him to take cover and wait until dark. I'll send an escort party out for him at nightfall.'

'But, Hunda, I——'

'Do as I say. Out.'

Avandir yelped and rubbed his ear as the radio emitted a blare of static. No arguing with the Major. Avandir felt like a student again. He unclipped the signalling lamp from his belt and flashed the message. Igin halted. He looked so lost and pathetically alone in the wasteland of ruined buildings.

His arm came up and waved three times, acknowledging the signal. Then Avandir saw him settle down in a shell hole, his back to a slab of masonry.

Poor beggar. Hours to wait before sundown. What was Hunda playing at? Igin was not a fit man. Dammit, he'd accomplished the mission, why make him wait?

Avandir broke open a biscuit ration and munched, watching the tiny grey figure all alone in the middle of nowhere.

Soolin pursed her lips and gazed at Vila with a puzzled frown. He was holding a shallow plastic tray at eye-level, his face creased in concentration. She said, 'You know, Vila, your obsession with that tray of dirt is beginning to bother me a little.'

'I've got the makings of a dozen wheatfields here,' Vila muttered. 'If I can get them to germinate.' He pushed the tray back into the cabinet on its sliding runners and rubbed his hands together, humming under his breath.

'I don't see you as the back-to-nature type somehow.' Soolin sat on the arm of the couch, her chin propped in the palm of her hand, watching him. She'd thought Vila the least complicated of her four new companions, but she was discovering that even he had depths she'd never suspected.

Vila said, 'If we're going to be here as long as Avon reckons, then we might as well be comfortable.' He looked wistful for a moment. 'I keep dreaming about toast.'

'Toast?' Soolin's parents had emigrated from Earth to the frontier world Darlon IV when she was two-years-old. The customs and traditions – and food – of the old planet were alien to her.

'A delicacy,' Vila explained. He kissed his fingertips.

'Report for Avon,' Orac said in his usual peremptory tone.

Soolin went across to where Orac sat on a low table. For the past hour his circuitry had been winking and flashing as if locked in deep metaphysical thought. 'What is it, Orac?'

'Report for Avon.'

Vila touched the contact on the wall communicator. 'Avon, your friend Orac wants a chat.' He released the contact and turned away. 'Some people dream about money or power. I dream about toast.'

'Hm.' Soolin was distinctly unenthralled. 'Well, unless you can make whatever that is out of pure dirt I should forget it.'

'There must be thousands of them in these trays – potentially,' Vila enthused. 'All I need is a mill and a bakery and a few slaves to do the work.'

'And some seeds that'll germinate,' Soolin said pragmatically.

Avon strode into the Crew Room followed by Dayna.

'What is it, Orac?'

'You asked me to report any extension of the Federation Command network,' the thinking machine reminded him crisply. 'Magnetrix Terminal four-zero-six is now programmed in.'

'What planet does the terminal serve?'

'Helotrix.'

Avon stared. 'I don't believe it!'

'It is the main terminal for the planet Helotrix.' Orac wasn't used to being contradicted. It upset his diodes. 'The fact is checked and confirmed.'

Avon looked gravely at the others. 'That means the Helots are back in the Empire – but they aren't the sort to cave in that quickly. It took the Federation years to subdue them on the first expansion.'

Dayna went to the hologram screen and punched up a multi-dimensional view of an S-shaped constellation, two of whose stars were circled in bright red. 'They've retaken Lubas and Porphyr Major in the last few weeks. If Helotrix has gone that means the Federation now controls most of Vector Four.'

Vila scowled. 'If they keep expanding at this rate, Avon, we haven't all the time you thought.' He looked gloomily at the hologram. 'They'll be knocking on the door in a couple of years.'

'How are they doing it?' Avon smacked his fist into his palm. 'How?'

'I don't know, but maybe we should start running now,' said Vila darkly. 'I always thought your idea of making this a combat base was crazy.'

'We've been running too long,' Avon said, staring at the hologram. 'No, we've *got* to find out what it is the Federation are doing – why the old colonies are being reconquered so easily.' His lips thinned. 'Then maybe we can do something to stop them.'

'The five of us?' Vila cackled. His eyebrows shot up. 'Oh, I was forgetting Trooper Orac here . . .'

Avon paced up and down. 'We need to know how they're doing it. There must be a new factor – a new weapon – something we don't know about.'

'All the more reason to start running,' Vila mumbled. 'Right now.'

'Oh drop it, Vila!' Dayna exploded. 'Avon's right.'

'If it *is* something new, how are we going to find out about it?' Soolin asked.

'There's only one way,' Avon replied. 'We have to go to Helotrix.'

'You're getting worse than Blake used to be!' Vila fumed. 'You're turning into a hero, Avon.'

'Whatever the occasion demands.' A slow grin crept over Avon's face. 'Actually, I'm going to let Tarrant be the hero. Soolin – tell him to get *Scorpio* ready for take-off.'

Chapter Eight

Colonel Quute leaned over the duty tracer's shoulder, watching the stationary green blip on the plot screen. 'You're sure?'

'Target hasn't moved in over an hour, sir. Steady as a rock.'

Quute straightened up, a broad bull of a man, and pulled the dark grey blouson-style tunic down at the back. The Federation insignia in bas-relief gleamed dully on his left breast. He debated for a moment and then said, 'Presumably Igin's got back to base. Right. Prepare for neutron strike.'

The duty tracer nodded at the two ordnance engineers manning the fire control board. A light blinked on and the duty tracer said: 'All launchers mobile, sir.'

Colonel Quute kneaded his fist. 'Ready launchers three and seventeen. Fifty metre bracket pattern.'

The ordnance engineers adjusted the controls, aligning the launchers to the required configuration.

'Three and seventeen locked on – now!' the duty tracer reported. 'Prepare for strike.'

'Primary relay open,' and, 'Safety lock clear,' said the two engineers almost together.

'Fire.' Quute's mouth snapped shut like a trap.

'Five and counting,' intoned the duty tracer. 'Four . . . three . . . two . . .'

Avandir blinked, trying to clear the bright orange after-image on the retina of his eyes. Where, only a moment ago, the tiny figure of Igin had been in the landscape of rubble, there was now a vast smoking crater. The explosion had shocked him more by its unexpectedness than its actual blast; his mind still reeling, he turned to Hunda, crouching grim-faced beside him in the angle of the shattered wall.

'They must have had some kind of marker on him.'

From Hunda's face, Avandir realised that the Major must have suspected something like this all along . . . wait until nightfall, he had said.

Hunda said bleakly, 'That should have been me. It was my idea.'

'Igin volunteered.' It sounded puny, but it was the truth.

'I should never have let him go.' Hunda turned away, his eyes hard and stony. 'He wasn't up to it.'

'But that's *why* he volunteered, Hunda – don't you see? He wanted to be of use!'

'All the same, it was my idea,' Hunda said, unwilling – or unable – to be comforted. 'I should have gone.'

'With any luck, sir, the rebels' fourth column has just ceased to exist,' Colonel Quute told the General. They were standing at the window of the missile launch blockhouse, which Quute was using as a temporary HQ.

'Well done, sir!' The General clapped him on the shoulder. He was a very tall, powerful man with a ram-rod bearing and a way of walking as though he had springs in his heels. He raised his silver-capped baton. 'Mind you,' he went on, 'I have a sneaking respect for these Helots. Yes indeed. Led a squadron of 'em once. Marvellous fighters, especially at close quarters.' He leaned forward an inch on the tips of his toes. 'They love the hand-to-hand stuff, you know.'

'Not really necessary, of course, these days,' said Colonel Quute with a rather wearisome smile. Which war did the fool think they were fighting? The First Occupation?

'Don't you believe it, Quute.' The General tapped his gloved palm with the baton. 'Can't do everything with your missiles. Bunkers! Strongpoints! Inter-city combat!' The baton thwacked leather, driving each point home. 'You've got to winkle 'em out with cold steel. Only way of clearing the ground.'

'Gas?' Quute proposed.

'Not always effective. Can't be sure of it. You remember the Fletch expedition of 'twenty-nine?'

Quute lifted one shoulder. 'No, I'm afraid——'

'Before your time, probably.' The General evidently did. Vividly. 'Fletch used gas against the Waazis. Complete massacre. Bodies everywhere. Took dinner with his officers that night and suddenly the Waazis came over the wall. Butchered the whole expedition.' The General snorted. 'It seems

Waazis are gill-breathers, do you see? They can lie dormant for days.'

'That's very interesting, sir,' Colonel Quute said politely.

'You'll send out a patrol to do a body-count?'

'Of course.'

'Don't use your own troops,' the General advised, tapping him on the chest. 'We've got some adapted Helots under training.'

'Yes, I've seen them, sir.'

'What do you think of 'em?' asked the General shrewdly.

'Well,' Quute shrugged, 'they seem like all Helots after adaptation – suggestible, obedient, glad to follow orders. They should make good troops.'

The General wasn't so convinced. 'Dunno. Something missing, I think.' His tiny eyes narrowed, his lower lip jutted. 'Fire in the belly, Quute. Can't fight without it.'

'No, sir.'

'Anyway, must be off.' The General waved his baton. 'I'm meeting the President-elect shortly.'

Colonel Quute walked him to the door, the General taking great care to step over the piles of rubbish so as not to smudge the shine on his gleaming knee-high boots.

'I heard Practor had arrived,' said Quute. 'He's a Helot, they say?'

The General nodded. 'Oh yes, born and bred. Good idea, don't you think, getting one of their own to run the place?'

'Is he adapted, sir?'

'Not necessary,' the General said briskly. 'Practor's been on the Federation Civil List for years. Absolutely reliable. Knows all the ropes, so it shouldn't be too long before we hand over, eh? Then we can get on to Uanta.'

Colonel Quute's face went wooden. 'Uanta?'

'That's our next assignment,' the General informed him cheerfully. 'Something to look forward to, eh?'

'Oh yes, sir!' said Colonel Quute with a show of enthusiasm. 'I'll look forward to that no end.'

He saluted as the General touched the baton to the peak of

his cap and went out. Then Colonel Quute turned and stormed across to the duty tracer.

'Where the blazes,' he demanded, 'is Uanta?'

Scorpio approached Helotrix in the plasma shadow of the system's star. It was a risky trajectory but vital if the old cargo freighter was to have a chance of eluding the Federation detectors and the busy traffic lanes used by the battle cruisers and pursuit ships. The remaining problem – in Avon's estimation the *real* problem – was how they were going to maintain station above the planet, within teleport distance, and stay undetected while Tarrant and Dayna went down to the surface on their scouting trip.

But first things first. Get them down in one piece (better still, in two pieces) and then think about it. 'How long before we make planetfall?' he asked Tarrant, who was at the flight control module.

'Just over two hours.'

'You'd better check out which gun clips you want. I'll take over.'

'Think I'll pass for a Helot?' Dayna asked Avon.

'No problem. When Helotrix was settled the old Stock Equalisation Act was still in force. Every Earth race had to be represented.'

Soolin glanced up, surprised. 'I didn't know Helots were originally from Earth.'

'Everyone came from Earth originally,' said Vila glibly. 'It's a well-known fact.'

'It's a well-known opinion, actually,' Soolin replied coolly, giving him a look.

'Most well-known facts are,' Tarrant said, stepping down onto the main deck.

Avon settled himself at the controls. 'But not in this case. Helotrix was one of the oldest colonies and the first to gain independence from the Empire.'

'Until the Federation grabbed it back,' Tarrant remarked. 'Come on, Dayna. Let's get kitted-out.'

Vila watched them head for the equipment lockers at the rear of flight deck. 'That fool is actually looking forward to it,' he muttered sourly. 'He can't wait to go snooping around Helotrix.'

'Good material, Tarrant.' Avon smiled ingenuously. 'One of the best.'

'He's not the man for the job,' Vila insisted. 'Tarrant has about as much subtlety as a Bulrasian warg-strangler.'

Soolin arched an eyebrow. 'Are you volunteering?' she asked him.

'Me – walk into the middle of a war?'

'The Federation have the Terminal, according to Orac,' Soolin pointed out.

Vila's tone was darkly dismissive. 'That doesn't mean the fighting's over.' He jabbed his finger at her. 'All I'm saying is Tarrant's going to walk straight into trouble and get himself killed or captured – preferably the first.'

'Happy little comrade, aren't you?' Avon murmured dryly.

'Only thinking of myself,' Vila said, with the devastating mixture of cowardice and honesty he was famous for. 'If Tarrant's dead he can't talk. But if the Federation find we're hanging around we'll have no chance – not with this ship. At least in the *Liberator* we could always outrun them.'

'Vila,' Avon said, trying hard to be patient, 'if the Federation's got some new weapon, the Helots will know all about it. Tarrant only has to ask a few questions in the right places. Even your average Bulrasian warg-strangler might manage that.'

'You think so?' Vila said caustically. 'Well, you'd better give him a list of questions and a map to find the right places.' And with that he stumped across to one of the crash-couches and threw himself down, turning his face to the bulkhead.

Soolin looked at Avon, who was busy checking readouts. 'He doesn't have a lot of time for Tarrant, does he?' she said in her husky voice.

'Well, Tarrant is brave, young and handsome. Three good reasons for Vila not to like him.'

'He has a point, all the same.'

'About Tarrant?'

'About this ship,' said Soolin, glancing round. 'It was never designed to tangle with Federation cruisers.'

'I'm working on that,' Avon said, intent on the readouts.

'You are?' Soolin's eyes widened.

'With Orac's help.' Avon nodded towards Orac on the nearby communications console. 'These freighters are equipped with short-burn boosters to help lift their payloads into orbit. Orac is figuring out how we can redesign them to give us extra in-flight speed.'

'I thought he was keeping unusually silent,' she said with a smile.

'Probably sulking. One of the almost human things about Orac is that he doesn't really like work.' Avon leaned across on one elbow. 'Orac?'

'Yes, Avon.'

'Any progress with the booster problem?'

Orac's circuitry flickered inside the transparent case. 'There has been no reply yet,' came the bland response.

'What do you mean, no reply?' Avon frowned.

'I passed the program to computers specialising in engineering design.'

'You mean you can't handle it yourself?'

'The art of leadership is delegation,' said Orac loftily.

Avon shook his head, bemused, and caught Soolin's eye, and they both burst out laughing.

The four men sat at the scarred table in the one remaining room of what had been a public library, listening raptly as their commander gave his briefing. Major Hunda's voice was low and terse, his eyes flat and cold in the deeply-lined hawkish face.

'They'll push out a patrol to check our casualties. You'll have the chance to catch them in the open for once. Bait the ground well, then deploy the rest of the column behind Surveillance Post 3. Any questions?'

Hask said, 'We'll be in the open too. If they send in gunships we'll be cut to pieces.' He was a year or two older than Hunda, a taciturn and rather morose forty-year-old whose civilian occupation had been construction engineer.

'Take them by surprise, hit hard, and they'll have no time to call in gunships,' said Hunda curtly. 'And then get out fast. All right?'

All around them, metal racks leaned at crazy angles, spilling their loads of dusty, begrimed books onto the floor littered with plaster and other debris. This had once been a stockroom, until the library received a direct hit. The sun, low in the sky, touched the jagged shards of glass in the splintered window-frame with glaring red highlights, throwing rosy streaks along one wall.

The four section leaders looked at one another, and Avandir said, 'Prisoners?'

'We don't take prisoners.' It was a bald statement of fact.

'You should be in command,' Hask insisted.

Major Hunda stood up. 'I'm passing command to you, Hask.' He began to strip off his camouflaged battle dress. 'You take over the column until I get back.'

'Hunda, won't you think again?' Avandir pleaded. His vivid blue eyes were clouded with anxiety. 'Do you have to go?'

'Yes,' said Hunda grimly. He was donning an old pair of workman's trousers which hung baggily on his tall, spare figure. 'If I'd gone in the first place Igin would still be alive.'

'And you might be dead,' Avandir muttered.

Hunda bent over, strapping a small calibre handgun to his calf. 'We're losing this war,' he stated bluntly. 'But if we can destroy the Magnetrix Terminal we might still have a chance. And it's our only chance. I have to go.'

'There are plenty of others, Hunda – I'm willing to try,' Avandir said, his eagerness tinged with desperation. He respected and admired Hunda more than any man he had ever known. The thought that they might lose him made the younger man sick inside.

Major Hunda straightened up and reached for a jacket with ragged sleeves and rents in the back. 'You're not a geologist. We need to know the best point from which to start the shaft, how long it will take to construct, what equipment is required. A dozen things that only an expert can decide.'

'That's true,' said Hask, watching the commander closely, 'but how are you going to get into the city? We haven't found an entrance yet that isn't swarming with Federation troopers.'

'That's right!' Avandir agreed. 'They probably got Igin on their detector screens before he'd gone fifty yards——'

'I'm going to swim in under the reactors.' Hunda pulled a grimy peaked cap down over his eyes. 'I doubt if they've thought of that.'

'I doubt it too,' Avandir said faintly. He looked wildly round at the others and then at the Major. 'That's an impossible swim, Hunda! Fifty metres, at least, under water in total blackness.' His voice rose shrilly. 'You'll never make it!'

'I think I can,' Hunda said quietly. He stood at the head of the table looking down at them, his eyes lost in shadow under the peaked cap. 'There are two points along that cooling outlet where it's possible to surface, and as long as I keep my face to the current I shall be heading in the right direction.'

The four men watched in silence as he moved to the empty door frame and stood there a moment, a shabby nondescript figure in the light of the setting sun.

'All right, Hask, you take over now. Get the column moving. If all goes well I'll be back tomorrow night.' He raised his hand in a brief salute, and was gone.

'Good luck!' Hask called out, while Avandir, not trusting himself to speak, simply stared at the empty doorway, his eyes like shiny blue stones.

Chapter Nine

A melodious warbling tone announced the arrival of the elevator in the High Chamber. Leitz padded forward, his soft-soled shoes shuffling across the marble floor, and turned the security key which activated the heavy bronze doors. He stood deferentially to one side as the General stepped smartly out, followed at a more dignified pace by a large, rotund man with a fat, moonlike face who was dressed in purple robes with the Federation crest dangling on a heavy gold chain round his neck. The crest was propped at an angle on the ponderous swell of his belly, like a dinner plate about to slide off a shelf.

'This is the High Chamber, Excellency.' The General gestured with his baton. 'Still furnished to the taste of your predecessor, but that's easily changed, of course.' He stiffened, as if noticing the subservient lurking figure for the first time. 'You are . . .?'

'My name is Leitz, General.' The voice was soft, persuasive, in keeping with a face of strong lines and a distinctly square jaw. 'Commissioner Sleer sent me to act as His Excellency President-Elect Practor's liaison officer.' He made a small formal bow to the big man, showing a pale narrow forehead with a black widow's peak.

'Good.' The General balanced on the balls of his feet. 'Remarkable person, Sleer. Thinks of everything.'

'I know they think very highly of Sleer at Federation Headquarters,' Practor intoned in his precise, fussy manner, sweeping forward importantly into the chamber, lavishly decorated in the Neo-Baroque style.

'So they should, so they should,' said the General, adding, to make his point clear, 'If it wasn't for Commissioner

Sleer's pacification programme my task force would still be bogged down five star systems back.'

Practor paused and looked down his nose. 'I've heard of this adaptation; how is it done exactly?'

'Some new wonder drug, isn't it, Leitz?' the General grunted.

Leitz stood rubbing his hands at chest-level. 'The Commissioner controls its manufacture, Excellency. It's injected by medical laser. It acts immediately and has no side-effects.'

'But it changes the personality?' Practor surmised.

'Not to any great extent, Excellency, no. It simply blocks the production of adrenalin. The result is that adapted natives no longer resist us.'

'And they continue to work normally?'

'Completely.' Leitz smiled, revealing strong shining teeth. 'In fact the work ethic is often reinforced.'

'Really?' Practor pouted his prissy belly-button of a mouth.

'Industrial production on Tarsias has risen nineteen per cent since the natives were adapted,' Leitz informed him importantly.

'That's very impressive. What proportion of Helots have been adapted so far?'

Leitz looked towards the General, who was examining the architecture. 'Oh, the majority I should think,' the General replied. He smiled crookedly. 'Commissioner Sleer doesn't waste time.'

Practor moved on, saying casually, 'It's simply that as my shuttle came over this afternoon I saw some explosions out to the east. It seemed that fighting was still going on.'

'Isolated pockets of resistance,' explained the General hastily. 'They're being mopped up rapidly now. You actually saw the destruction of a rebel unit.'

Practor was examining a large wall hanging abstractedly. 'I didn't see any sign of life,' he said.

'They're very skilled at using cover. But we employed a live target for that particular strike.'

'A live target, General?' Practor said, looking down at him.

The General was on safer ground now. 'Oh yes. Sleer's people picked up a rebel who'd been sent in on an intelligence mission. He was adapted, given a tracer to swallow, and sent back to rejoin his friends. When he reached their base my missile commander just pressed the button.'

'Very ingenious.' Practor nodded, his cold eyes gleaming.

'And effective.' Stepping back a pace so that his steel heel caps resounded on the marble floor, the General said, 'I'll leave you now, Excellency, with your permission. We'll meet tomorrow at the swearing-in ceremony.'

'Thank you, General.' Practor waved a white flaccid hand on which a ruby ring gleamed like the embers of a fire. 'I'm most grateful to you.'

The General touched the peak of his cap with his baton, about-turned and marched to the elevator. When it had whined into silence, His Excellency President-Elect Practor began to inspect his new domain with an almost sensual anticipation, accompanied by the whispering shuffle of softly-shod feet.

Two things Hunda hadn't reckoned on: the heat of the water and the strength of the current. Under ideal conditions, with the current aiding him, the swim would have been difficult, but this was like trying to claw his way up a boiling hot waterfall, and almost as impossible.

That's what Avandir had called it – impossible – and Hunda was beginning to believe he was right.

And there was another mind-numbing thought that only now occurred to him. *What if he missed the cooling outlet?* What if he swam past it in the pitch blackness? Then he'd be trapped deep underground in a pipe filled with water, becoming hotter every second . . .

Hunda swam on with huge powerful strokes, every fibre of his body screaming for oxygen. His eyes were bulging with the internal pressure of holding the breath in his straining lungs. Several times his hand struck the smooth steel wall of the pipe, making his stomach muscles knot with the effort of suppressing the pain. But still he kept on, steadily beating the water behind him, knowing that if he panicked he was as good as dead.

The water was getting hotter, the current stronger. He must be nearly there – he must be! He reached upwards but could feel only the smooth rounded pipe. A pulse started to throb in his neck, as if it might rupture. Another agonising stroke, and then another, and he could feel the strength ebbing from his arms as the last few cubic inches of oxygen were used up.

He tried again, reaching upwards with manic desperation, and burst through the water, his fingers clawing to get a grip on the iron ladder bolted to the wall of the narrow concrete shaft.

For several minutes Hunda clung weakly to the ladder, sucking air into his tortured lungs. The roaring in his head gradually diminished and he was able to drag himself from the water and begin the long slow climb up the shaft.

He had achieved the impossible. He was inside the Magnetrix Terminal!

A quadrant of the planet filled the scanner. On the curvature of the rim, a soft blue-green haze faded into the dense blackness of space.

Somewhere beyond the scanner's view, the system's sun blazed with a hard pure light, bringing a new day to the continents and oceans directly below *Scorpio*.

'We are now holding station forty miles above the surface. I do hope this is satisfactory, Master.'

Avon said, 'So this is your big moment, Tarrant.' He was standing by the teleport control console, which was directly in front of the teleport bay itself.

'If the teleport works,' Tarrant said, taking two bracelets from the rack and handing one to Dayna. They were both wearing handguns and had a plentiful supply of magazine clips in their zippered arm pouches.

'It's working perfectly now,' Vila said cheerfully. 'I checked it myself.'

'But would you use it yourself, Vila?' Dayna grinned at him. 'That's the real test.'

'Ah, get in there and disappear!' Vila retorted, winking at Soolin.

Avon seated himself at the control console. 'Remember, Tarrant, we're only interested in one thing – whether the Federation's using some new kind of weapon. Whatever's happening down there, even if they're executing the whole population, you're not to get involved. All right?'

'Sure.' The slim curly-headed pilot nodded and stepped up beside Dayna in the teleport bay.

'Report when you're on the surface,' Avon said, operating the controls.

The faces of the three people watching were bathed in a rapidly flickering blue light as the outlines of Tarrant and Dayna became blurred and then fragmented into nothing.

Strictly speaking, only two were watching: Avon impassively, Soolin round-eyed and open-mouthed, while Vila had his eyes shut tight and his fingers crossed on both hands.

They materialised in a rubble-strewn ruin. Dark narrow streets where the houses had either been knocked flat or partially destroyed and boarded up. Smoke curled from broken chimneys and holes in the roofs, so presumably the unfortunate citizens of the Magnetrix Terminal still lived in them.

With a war ravaging their planet, they had little choice, Tarrant thought bleakly. He beckoned to Dayna and they slid into an alley, out of sight of the main street. Luckily there were few people about.

Here and there among the ruins, nature had begun to reassert itself: clumps of weird rubbery-looking plants with dark spotted leaves and long mossy creepers clinging to the concrete and brickwork as if trying to strangle the buildings. This was ugly, perverted nature, mirroring the gloomy devastation of its surroundings.

Making sure they were unobserved, Tarrant raised the bracelet to his mouth and said in a low voice, 'Tarrant to *Scorpio*. We're on the surface.'

He listened intently for several moments, then said to Dayna, 'Did you get an acknowledgement?'

She shook her head. 'Not a whisper.'

He tried again. 'Tarrant to *Scorpio*. Please say if you're receiving us.'

They listened to total silence. There wasn't even the hiss of static.

Dayna glanced round morbidly and shivered slightly. 'Looks as though we're stuck here, Tarrant. I knew I should have brought my nightclothes.'

'Well, they'll obviously be working on the fault. Nothing we can do about it.' He peered out carefully in the direction of the main street and then beckoned to her. 'Come on, let's go.'

On the flight deck Avon repeated the acknowledgement for the third time. Tarrant had come through loud and clear, but evidently he himself hadn't.

'I fear the sensors indicate audio malfunction.'

'Tell us something we don't know, Slave,' Vila snapped, exasperated.

'I do apologise most profoundly if I have given offence. I assure you that——'

'All right, Slave, shut up.' Avon sighed and got to his feet. 'Let's check the audio-beam,' he said to Vila, who raised his eyes and hands to heaven.

'Then from your private suite back into the reception chamber,' Leitz murmured, hovering like a satellite round Practor as they returned from the tour of inspection. 'Over here, Excellency——' the smooth-spoken man crept forward, hand outstretched '——is a communication centre which gives you video contact with any part of Helotrix. You also have a direct audio link, via the Magnetrix Terminal, with Federation Headquarters.'

'Not exactly "direct" then, is it, Leitz?' Practor said primly.

'No, Excellency.' Leitz coughed discreetly. 'I meant that it is private and priority-coded for your own exclusive use.'

Practor smiled and waved his hand carelessly. 'Don't worry, Leitz. It's simply that years in the civil service have turned me into something of a pedant.'

He moved across to an alcove hidden behind heavy velvet drapes from ceiling to floor and touched a button. The drapes parted to reveal a spot-lit life-sized portrait. Practor laced his fingers across his huge stomach and gazed up admiringly. 'Supreme Empress Servalan,' he said in a tone of reverent awe.

Leitz drifted up silently to stand beside him, his alert eyes taking in every inch of the canvas. 'Servalan . . .?' His eyes flickered towards Practor and back to the portrait of the beautiful young woman attired in a magnificent uniform and swathed in black furs. Feet braced apart, a white-gloved hand on one hip, she looked down on them with an imperious glacial arrogance that seemed to send a chill into the room. 'Is Your Excellency certain?' Leitz asked in a hushed voice.

'Of course.' Practor's face softened in a smug half-smile. 'I knew her well in the old days. Killed in the rearguard action at Geddon, I believe.'

'I knew she was reported dead, sir. I never heard any details.'

'There was a great deal of confusion when the High Council was restored to power. Most of the Old Guard were killed in the fighting. They remained loyal to Servalan right to the end.'

'And a lot of them were executed later, weren't they, sir? All the leaders were purged.'

Practor nodded sagely. 'The penalty for choosing the wrong side, Leitz. I myself was under arrest for a short time.'

Leitz looked up at the portrait, the corners of his thin-lipped mouth curving upwards. 'Well,' he murmured silkily, as if to himself, 'I suppose it's better to die bravely on the field than to face execution.'

Hunda, the peaked cap jammed down to his ears, hands thrust into the damp pockets of his torn jacket, arrived at the open square with its columns and pedestals just as the overhead speakers blared out deafeningly:

'Attention, citizens! Attention! This is a census! Leave the concourse now. Leave by Exits One and Three only. I repeat, Exits One and Three only.'

After only a momentary hesitation, people in the square began moving obediently to the exits, forming shuffling lines. Glancing over his shoulder, Hunda slipped behind a column, pressing close to the front of the building. Just his bad luck to get——

He froze, his attention caught by a young man and a woman who were standing indecisively at the corner of the square. Unlike the rest of the shabbily-dressed population, they wore one-piece combat-style coveralls and even had handguns strapped to their waists. Hunda watched as they backed away, looking furtively in every direction.

Tarrant touched Dayna's shoulder and jerked his head. 'Quick, back the way we came, down the alley . . .'

They turned and strode towards the narrow opening, and then pulled up dead. A visored guard appeared from the alleyway, a weapon with a bulbous nozzle cradled across his chest, and planted himself there, blocking the exit.

'Any ideas?' said Tarrant tersely from the corner of his mouth.

'Only one,' Dayna said, her fingers straying down to her handgun. 'We'll just have to go through him.'

Her hand closed round the butt and fingers clamped her

81

wrist in an iron grip and a voice said softly, 'That's what they're expecting, friends.'

Tarrant spun round. Before he could speak the man held up a cautioning hand. 'Follow me.' Without looking back, the man set off across the square in the general direction taken by the docile inhabitants. Tarrant and Dayna exchanged glances and began to follow the hunched figure in the ragged coat.

On the far side of the square, which had been badly damaged in the fighting, he ducked through a stone-fronted doorway into the ruins of a bombed house. The doorway and a crumbling knee-high wall were all that remained – the 'inside' was overgrown with weeds and the sinuous mossy creepers which seemed gradually to be taking over the city.

Dayna scrambled after him into the pungent, dank undergrowth, shuddering slightly. Behind her, Tarrant nearly tripped and cursed under his breath. A moment later all three were crouching in a dark green twilight and peering out through the dense shrubbery.

'We'll lie low until the check's over.' The man removed his cap and wiped his forehead with his sleeve. 'They can't search the whole concourse.'

'What's the check for?' Dayna asked, glimpsing a deeply-lined face with a hawkish profile in the dimness.

'Catching people like us – the unadapted,' said Hunda.

'Unadapted?' Tarrant said curiously. 'What do you mean?'

Hunda eyed them both keenly. 'You're off-worlders, aren't you?'

Tarrant said, 'You got us right the first time. We're friends – of anyone fighting the Federation.'

'What's this about people like us being unadapted?' Dayna wanted to know.

Before Hunda could answer a man dashed across the square towards them. He leapt over the low wall and fell to his knees amongst the overgrown rubble, breathing hoarsely, his face drenched with sweat. The visored head of a guard appeared, the bulbous muzzle of his weapon levelled. Frantically, the man lurched to his feet and staggered backwards to where the three hidden watchers were crouching, hardly daring to breathe.

Another guard stepped over the wall and circled round, closing in. The hunted man looked round desperately, seeking an escape route. He was less than ten feet away from the hiding-place when Tarrant's bracelet began beeping its call signal. Tarrant jabbed the button, muffling it at once.

Realising he was cut off, the man turned and lunged for the deep undergrowth, and very calmly one of the guards raised his weapon and lanced him between the shoulder blades with a silent, needle-thin laser beam. The effect was astonishing. The man stopped, arms outstretched, and the terrified panic on his face was transformed into a vague bewildered frown, as if he'd just awoken from a dream and had no idea where he was or what he was doing there.

Taking him by the arm, the guard led him back through the rubble to the square. The dazed man stood gazing into space while the two guards examined his papers, then prodded him with the strange-looking weapons in the direction of the checkpoint.

Hunda released a pent-up sigh of relief and sank back. Dayna glanced across at Tarrant, who nodded, grimacing at his bracelet. 'Avon certainly chooses his moments,' he said dourly.

'At least they've fixed the teleport,' Dayna said. 'And we've had a demonstration of the Federation's new weapon.'

'Isn't there any defence against it?' Tarrant asked.

'Only to shoot first,' Hunda said briefly. He pulled his cap on and parted the packed shrubbery, squinting out. 'We can move in a few minutes. They won't run another census today.' He looked at them. 'But in those outfits you won't get fifty yards. We'll have to find you some clothes.'

Vila leaned over the communication console, pointing his finger in Avon's face. 'What did I say? Didn't I *tell* you Tarrant would blow it?'

'We don't know that for certain,' Soolin said mildly, sitting with arms crossed on the corner of the chart table, swinging her legs.

'Right now,' Vila went on, incensed, 'he's probably strung up by the ears while they thread red-hot filaments through his nerve-centres – if he's got any. Then it'll be: where are you from? How did you get here? Are there any more at home like you?' He thumped the console. 'For pity's sake, Avon, get this ship moving while we still have the chance.'

'Slave,' Avon called out. 'I want an infra-red surface scan every thirty seconds. Immediate notification of any launchings——'

'That'll be too late!' Vila moaned, clenching his fists impotently.

'I don't think so.' Avon inspected his fingernails, completely unperturbed by Vila's outburst. 'As Soolin says, we can't be sure that anything's happened to them.'

'Maybe it just wasn't convenient for them to answer,' the blonde girl shrugged.

'Right!' Vila agreed heatedly, swinging round to face her. 'Like, for instance, their arms are being pulled off at the shoulder.'

'Vila,' Avon said, his voice clipped. 'Until we're attacked, we're staying. Is that clear?'

'Blake would have been proud of you, you know,' said Vila scathingly.

'I know. But then he never was very bright,' Avon said with a smile that might have been chipped off an iceberg.

Practor sat hunched before the angled screen inset into the desk. A single light burned on a slender aluminium stalk above, making black circles of his eyes. Blocks of data raced past. Practor tapped the silver stylus on the desk-top, made a notation, tapped again.

He raised his head at the sound of the mellow warbling tone. Frowned. Pressed an actuator with a fat finger.

A pleasant female voice said, 'House Computer. You require?'

'You've allowed access to my private elevator. To whom?'
'Commissioner Sleer to see Your Excellency.'

Practor swung round in the swivel chair and heaved his bulk upright. He moved hurriedly across the darkened chamber, turned the security key, and stepped forward, straightening his robes and chain of office, anxious to greet his important visitor. This was indeed a rare honour.

The bronze doors sighed open and Practor's carefully arranged expression sagged like jelly, smearing his features into blank disbelief. His small pouting lower lip trembled.

'You! But – but how——'

From inside the elevator came the sharp explosive crack of a neutron bolt.

Practor gurgled, coughed, choked, and sank slowly to his knees. Blood seeped from the corner of his mouth. He went cross-eyed and fell face down on the marble floor with a dull hollow clunk.

Soundlessly, the robed figure glided across the chamber. Another neutron bolt blasted the teledata screen to smithereens. Without pausing the figure turned towards the alcove, operated the drapes, and aimed a third bolt at the centre of the portrait. A large black hole appeared and spread outwards, the paint peeling and sizzling. Burning fragments drifted down leaving tiny smoking trails.

The figure returned to the elevator. The doors closed. The whine of hydraulics faded and the darkened chamber was silent once more.

Chapter Ten

Face streaked with dirt and dressed in a shapeless suit, which effectively concealed his combat drill and the bulge of his handgun, Tarrant leaned with his back to the makeshift bar and casually surveyed the dozen or so Helots drinking at the crude tables. There was minimal conversation. No laughter, no smiling faces. And no wonder in this joyless hole, Tarrant thought, with its bare brick walls and sheet metal roof. The place had the depressing austerity of a demoralised, defeated people.

For the sake of appearances he took a swig of the weak amber liquid they called beer, and had to tense his stomach muscles to prevent him spewing it out again. Next to him at the bar, Hunda finished his off with apparent relish and crumpled the cardboard cup and dropped it onto the filthy floor.

Hardly moving his lips, Tarrant said, 'No sign of him?'

Hunda gave a barely perceptible shake of the head and leaned nonchalantly with one elbow on the scratched wooden bar-top, covering his mouth with a grimy hand. 'In the first weeks of the occupation this was always our meeting-point. But maybe he's stopped coming.'

'Don't you have any other way of contacting him?' Dayna asked. 'I mean, just turning up here at this time of day——' She shrugged under the long sacklike grey shift, the standard garment for women, which added another forty pounds to her figure. 'Seems a bit haphazard.'

'We never had time to get organised,' Hunda explained.

'So you've had no contact with other resistance units?' murmured Tarrant.

'None.' Hunda's flat grey eyes flicked across the few pathetic customers sunk in their own lethargy. 'Maybe mine's the only column still fighting.'

Someone came into the bar and Hunda stiffened. The newcomer went to collect a drink in a cardboard cup and stood sipping it, staring vacantly at nothing.

'Is that Leitz?' Dayna said alertly.

Hunda nodded. 'Did I give it away?'

The man appeared to notice Hunda for the first time and came up, his pale forehead with it's widow's peak distinctive even in this dim light. The two men clasped elbows. After a brief exchange of greetings Hunda led the way to a table against the wall. 'My friends, Dayna and Tarrant,' he introduced them. 'They're from Earth – but enemies of the Federation.'

Leitz nodded to each in turn and was about to speak when Hunda went on urgently, 'Tell me, Leitz – have you any news from the other columns?'

'Nothing good.' Leitz shook his head sombrely. 'Two's been practically wiped out. One and three have suffered heavy casualties and have pulled back into the White Mountains to regroup.'

'So mine's the only unit still functioning?'

'And you can expect to come under heavy attack in the next few days,' Leitz told him. 'The General is getting impatient.'

'We beat off their last attack. Shot down two gunships.'

'I heard. How did you get into the city, Hunda?'

'I swam under the reactors.'

Leitz paused with the cardboard cup halfway to his lips and stared. 'I'm sorry you took such a risk to hear bad news.'

'That wasn't why I came.' Hunda glanced round. He said in a low voice, 'I wanted to see how far the flood level had fallen.'

Leitz looked puzzled. 'Why?'

'I hoped we might tunnel in from the lower city and lay mines under the Magnetrix Terminal. But the flood water's too high.' For Dayna and Tarrant's benefit he added, 'In the first days of the fighting we blew the reservoirs.'

Dayna said, 'The Terminal is their communication centre?'

'Yes. If we could knock it out they'd be isolated.'

'Couldn't you infiltrate an assault group?' Tarrant asked. 'Or is it too heavily defended?'

'It's not defended at all,' Leitz replied. 'But they've got the city sealed off . . .' His voice trailed away and he sat there with a frown on his broad face, like a thoughtful bear.

'What is it?' Hunda said.

Leitz beat a little tattoo on the table. 'Something I just remembered . . . sealed off.' He looked up quickly. 'They sealed off the old monorail about a hundred years ago. Hunda, if you could find it——'

'I know where it runs,' said Hunda, thinking hard. 'It's still shown on the plans.'

'You could bring an army along there – right into the heart of the city!' Leitz said in a soft urgent voice.

'You're right!' Hunda gripped the edge of the table. 'We could destroy the Terminal and their Command HQ in one strike! By God, we'll win this war yet!'

'Careful,' Leitz warned, his eyes shifting round. 'You're not acting adapted.'

Hunda subsided, but it was clear he was bursting to put the scheme into effect. It would be a master stroke. 'Listen, I must get back to my column. We'll attack at dawn.' He stood up and pulled on his cap. 'I don't suppose we'll meet again,' he said to Tarrant and Dayna. 'I hope you get the information you need.' He gave them a grim smile and turned away, and then glanced back for a moment. 'Oh – and Leitz.'

'Yes?'

'Remember to keep your head down when we come in tomorrow. I wouldn't like to lose you after all the valuable work you've done.'

Leitz smiled and watched him leave, then looked keenly at the other two. 'What's this information you need?'

Tarrant said, 'We've been sent to learn what we can about the new drug the Federation's using.'

'Pylene-50?' Leitz looked carefully around. 'What do you want to know?'

'Everything,' said Dayna. 'Where's it manufactured?'

'Here.'

'The drug is actually made here on Helotrix?'

Leitz nodded. 'It has to be. Pylene-50 only remains stable for a few days, then the enzyme bonds break up and it's no longer effective.'

Tarrant chewed his lower lip. 'Dayna, if we could get hold of a sample for analysis . . .' He bent towards Leitz. 'Where's the synthesising plant?'

'Not far from here. I could show you. But it's guarded night and day.'

'Worth taking a look, Tarrant,' Dayna said, raising her eyebrows.

'I wouldn't leave without.'

'Well, be careful,' said Leitz, his face breaking into a worried frown. 'I'd come with you but I can't stay any longer.'

Tarrant grasped his shoulder. 'You've been a great help already, Leitz. We're both very grateful.'

Leitz smiled and crumpled the cardboard cup in his small fist.

The duty tracer couldn't understand it. Probably because it didn't make sense.

For the past two hours he'd been laboriously monitoring routine traffic on the screen: troop deployment, supply quotas, flight vectors, communications signals between Federation HQ and Magnetrix Terminal – all the usual stuff. It was late and he was tired, so at first he didn't pay much attention to the rows of mathematical data zipping by at eye-blink speed.

When he did decide to, he couldn't make head nor tail of it. What the hell was going on? As near as he could judge, this was classified technical information.

Wide awake now, the duty tracer cleared the screen and keyed in:

TL–73 PROGRAM AUTHTY?

The computer replied:

TL–73 AUTHTY ORAC

That didn't make sense either. At once the duty tracer put out a priority call for Colonel Quute. Then, on his own initiative, he began to conduct a scan on full power, seeking to locate the source of the mysterious signal. There it was, large as life, appearing as a dancing green blob in the middle of the screen. The damn thing wasn't stable, though. He tried for fine resolution and the blob started to oscillate wildly. By the time Colonel Quute arrived with the General in tow he'd lost it altogether.

The duty tracer briefed them, and the Colonel said, 'Did you fix its position?' He was breathing hard and the top buttons of his dark-grey tunic were undone, as if he'd donned it on the run.

'Not enough time, sir. But it's above Roche's Limit, so it must be a spacecraft.'

'Or a spy satellite,' Quute growled, kneading a meaty fist.

'What's the thing called?' asked the General, squinting at the blank screen. 'Orac?'

'Yes, sir.'

'Means nothing to me.' The General turned to Quute. 'What was the data it was taking from the Terminal?'

'A study on freighter design modifications. It was information being relayed from Space Centre.'

The General sniffed and clasped his hands behind his back. 'Sounds like a spot of commercial jiggery-pokery to me, Quute. Shouldn't fret over it.'

Colonel Quute resisted the urge to sigh. 'That's not really the point, sir,' he said tightly.

'These spaceship consortia are always at each other's throats. Underhand bunch. I could tell you some stories, Quute.'

'Yes, sir, but——'

'Most of them are Skellerians, you know,' the General confided, having found a favourite topic. 'Utter rogues, the lot of 'em. Corruption's a way of life. Slimy bunch. Can't fight worth a damn, either,' he snorted derisively.

'But, General, this is a *security* problem,' Quute was at pains to point out. If only his superior officer would stick to the point. 'It means that whatever's up there must be able to draw information from data-banks anywhere in the Federation.'

The General stared at him, stroking his chin. 'Really?'

'Yes, sir.'

'What——' the General waved his hand in circles '——troop movements, that sort of thing? Important stuff?'

Quute nodded gravely. 'An open book, General.'

'Then dammit, Quute!' the General barked, thrusting his shoulders back and straightening up. 'We must put a stop to it! At once!'

'Yes, sir. If you would authorise a search-and-destroy mission——'

'Absolutely.' The General paced the room, hands behind his back. 'These damn Skellerians poke their long noses into everything. Beastly greasy beggars . . .'

Colonel Quute closed his eyes. And sighed.

'What are these, Orac?' Avon inquired, studying the lines of mathematical symbols flashing by on the screen.

'Coefficient factors of nose-cone profiles.'

'All right. File them. What's the next program?'

'Weight and velocity indices.'

'File those too. In fact, store all the data. I'll go through it when we get back to base.'

'*If* we get back to base.' Lounging on the crash-couch, hands behind his head, Vila craned his neck to stare moodily across the flight deck. 'How much longer are we going to wait, Avon?'

It was the slim blonde girl who gave the tart reply, 'Until we get the information we came for.'

Vila sniggered. 'You're an optimist, Soolin.'

'And you're a very poor judge of character.'

'Vila's not at his best hanging around,' Avon told her, dead-pan. 'He's an action man.'

Vila sat up and took to jabbing his finger once again. 'I'll tell you what kind of man I am, Avon – I'm a running man. The way you used to be before you caught terminal

Blakeitis.' His expression of disgust was wasted on Avon, who was still watching the screen. Vila went 'Pah!' and dropped back into his former position and glared at the ceiling.

Soolin rested her crossed arms on the flight control module and propped her chin on them, gazing at Avon with a glint of sly amusement in her lovely eyes. 'I suppose it isn't possible that you and Blake do have something in common after all?' she said huskily.

'No, it isn't,' Avon said, watching the screen. 'We're different in every possible way.'

'For instance?' Soolin said archly.

'For instance, I survived.' Avon looked at her. 'Blake didn't.'

Looking round the High Chamber and speaking into the wall communicator handset, Leitz said deferentially, 'No, Commissioner. The video system's been completely destroyed.'

He grimaced and moved his ear away as the voice crackled over what was a very bad line. 'All right, Leitz. See nothing's touched. And inform the General.'

'I have done, Commissioner. He's on his way.'

'Good. Tell him I'll take charge of the investigation personally. We need an arrest before Headquarters are told of Practor's death.'

'Of course, Commissioner.'

There was a loud electronic burp as the line went dead. Wincing, Leitz hung up and closed the speaker panel. Rubbing his ear, he hurried towards the elevator in response to the melodious warble and turned the key to admit the General who was accompanied by two troopers in their leather uniforms and black-tinted visors.

The General gripped the baton in both gloved hands, turning his entire body while he gave the wrecked room his professional scrutiny. Then he bent over the body lying in a pool of dried blood. 'Neutron bolt. Somebody wanted to make very sure of him, eh?' He reached down to roll the body over.

Leitz coughed deprecatingly. 'Commissioner Sleer said to touch nothing, sir.'

The General straightened up at once. 'Sleer's taking charge, eh?'

'Yes, sir.'

'Well, it is a police job, I suppose.' The General tugged at the lobe of his ear. 'You've searched the private suite?'

'Yes, General.'

'Practor must have let him in, so the killer's somebody he knew, presumably. I'd say that limits the field somewhat . . .' He glanced sharply at Leitz. 'Where were you when he was killed?'

'I had to meet somebody in the concourse,' said Leitz smoothly.

'So the killer could have seen you leave and knew Practor was alone?'

'It's possible, sir.'

The General nodded and moved a few paces into the chamber while he cogitated on this. Abruptly he spun round on one heel. 'Of course you can prove that you had this meeting?'

Leitz opened his mouth and closed it again. He said slowly, 'That might be difficult.'

The General's eyes narrowed suspiciously. 'Why?'

'Because my meeting was with Hunda, General. And two off-worlders.'

A nervous tic jumped in the General's right cheek. His colour changed. 'What the blazes are you talking about, man?' he roared. 'Hunda is a rebel leader!'

'Yes, he managed to get into the city. You see,' Leitz went on to explain matter-of-factly, 'from the time you landed here I've been co-ordinating the resistance. I've kept in contact with all the rebel columns. They trust me.'

The General nearly choked. His neck swelled over his stiff collar.

'This is treason, Leitz! You could be shot out of hand!'

Leitz shook his head and smiled. He was very like a cat. Very softly, he murmured, 'Not for what I've done, General. It was Commissioner Sleer's idea that I should keep in touch with the rebels so that we'd have advance knowledge of their plans.'

'You mean you're some sort of filthy double-spy, is that it?'

'It was my information that led to the destruction of their second column,' Leitz said, unperturbed. He added smoothly, 'And Hunda's column is about to walk into a similar trap.'

The General breathed in. 'Go on.'

'He's planning a raid on the Magnetrix Terminal.' Leitz crept forward, grinning. 'At dawn he'll enter the city by the old monorail tunnel. Once his column's inside the tunnel all you have to do is blow it in, General.'

'Blow it in.' The General rubbed the back of his neck. 'That's all we have to do . . .' He frowned. He was evaluating this new possibility. It had promise. 'Yes. I suppose so.'

'It'll finish resistance once and for all!' Leitz insisted.

'You mentioned two off-worlders at this meeting?'

'They're interested in the adaption drug.' Leitz gave a grim smile. 'I sent them to the laboratory – though naturally I didn't tell them about our security measures.'

'Naturally,' said the General distastefully.

Leitz rubbed his hands. 'I expect they're dead now.'

The General had to turn away. He couldn't stand that smile a moment longer.

Chapter Eleven

Bored with guard duty, his thoughts light-years away, the Federation trooper's reactions were painfully slow. He unslung the weapon from his shoulder and was still fumbling with the safety catch when the muffled *thunk* from Tarrant's handgun spelled oblivion. The trooper tottered backwards and slid down the wall, head askew, legs splayed out.

Tarrant stepped over him to examine the locking mechanisms of the laboratory door. 'Photo-cell,' he said briefly over his shoulder.

Dayna unzipped the trooper's pockets and delved inside. 'Here.' She held up a plastic key. Tarrant took it from her and turned back to the door as she dragged the body out of sight. Something metallic tinkled to the ground.

'Tarrant – wait!' Dayna examined the small perforated metal plate. 'What do you make of this?'

Tarrant bent down to look. His jaw hardened. 'It's a pin-code.' His eyes held hers for a moment. They'd nearly walked into a trap. He straightened up and looked round thoughtfully at the stonework adjacent to the door. 'They usually hide the gate some distance away.'

It took them a minute to find it: a plastic cover simulated to look like stone which opened to reveal a metal box bristling with pins. The metal plate fitted precisely, and under steady pressure pushed the pins not lined up with the perforations flush with the base of the box. 'Just saved our lives, I think,' Tarrant said with a rueful grin.

Together they searched the door surround. 'This must be booby-trapped, Tarrant,' Dayna said, and then spotted the tiny vents along the top and down the sides. 'There!'

'Yes, that was the trick,' Tarrant nodded grimly. 'Gas diffusers.'

'Nerve gas?'

'Or something worse.' Tarrant inserted the plastic key and gingerly turned it. 'Now, let's pray there isn't a back-up system . . .'

Holding his breath, he eased the door ajar. They waited tensely. Tarrant breathed a sigh of relief. 'So far so good.' He pushed the door open. 'Ladies first.'

'You're so gallant,' murmured Dayna, drawing her handgun and stepping inside.

95

The laboratory was in darkness. There were long workbenches loaded with complex apparatus, gleaming faintly, and all around the pungent smell of chemicals. From somewhere came the steady drip of water, emphasising the silence. Obviously the place had closed down for the night.

Suddenly light flooded from above. Blinking in its harsh glare, Tarrant and Dayna swung round, handguns levelled. But whatever they had been expecting, it wasn't this.

The man in the wheelchair was diminutive, hunched, and completely hairless, without eyebrows or eyelashes. His skin was a kind of dead-looking pasty white. A pair of mauve spectacles darkened his eyes. His hands, resembling the claws of a bird, were bunched in his lap, and from them a wire trailed to the floor and disappeared into a dark recess under one of the benches.

'Under my hand there is an electrical contact. If it closes it will detonate seven hundred kilos of glyceryl trinitrate.' The voice that issued through the dry flaking lips was a toneless whine. It was a perfect match for the rheumy eyes sunk deep in their sockets. 'Put your guns away.'

Tarrant and Dayna exchanged looks and slowly holstered their weapons.

Dayna said lightly, 'Nitro-glycerine's a bit outdated, isn't it?'

'It was all I could make with my somewhat limited resources. And it is still a highly effective explosive.' The man paused and leaned back in the wheelchair. 'You're not from the Federation, I gather?'

Tarrant shook his head.

'Your surreptitious entry was enough to tell me that. Who are you and where are you from?' When they hesitated, the man went on in a voice that was less shrill, 'Come now. I may be friendlier than you think.'

'My name is Dayna. This is Tarrant. We're Federation outlaws.'

The tiny bespectacled head nodded slowly. 'Yes, I remember those names – there was a reward for your capture.

You and your friends have a ship called the *Liberator*, am I right?'

'We had,' Tarrant said bluntly. 'Past tense. *Liberator* was destroyed.'

'Memory is one of the few faculties I have that still functions perfectly. My name, by the way, is Forbus.'

'Forbus . . . you're not really going to press that contact, are you?' Tarrant said uneasily. 'The explosion would kill you too.'

Forbus opened his hands on the small black device with the single red button. 'That would seem a waste at the present time,' he agreed, placing the device on a bench-top. 'When I die I want Commissioner Sleer right beside me.'

'But you work for Sleer,' Dayna exclaimed. 'Manufacturing Pylene-50 . . .'

Forbus gripped the padded leather arms, his thin knuckles showing through the white dead skin. 'I'm compelled to work for Sleer – the inhuman devil! This wheelchair . . . my condition . . . Sleer's responsible for what you see!' His eyes roamed vaguely about the room. 'And now only Sleer keeps me alive.'

'What do you mean?' asked Tarrant curiously. 'What happened, Forbus?'

Forbus went on to explain in his weak high-pitched voice, as if he were describing a rather dull laboratory experiment to a class of students.

'Pylene-50, used homeopathically, is a muscle relaxant. Sleer discovered that at a hundred times' normal dosage it subverts the will, and tried to force me to part with the formula. I refused. I didn't understand Sleer's nature then . . . the totally callous, savage ambition. There's a poison called tincture of pyrhennic. Perhaps you've heard of it? No matter. It's the extract of Pamporanian fungi. It cripples and eventually kills. Death is agonising and there is no cure. I have pyrhennic poisoning: Sleer's doing.'

There was a silence, broken by Dayna's hushed voice. 'You mean you're dying?'

'There is an antidote that prevents the poison spreading. As long as I take it daily I get no worse. Sleer, of course, controls my supply.'

Tarrant stared at the hunched, emaciated figure, weighing no more than a child. 'So long as you continue to manufacture Pylene-50?'

'That's the threat always over my head,' Forbus said with a wan smile. 'Work for Sleer or die in agony. But from time to time the Commissioner calls in here to taunt me. To gloat.' He eyed the device on the bench. 'Now, with my outdated nitro-glycerine, Dayna, I am ready. I hope Leitz comes as well. He usually does,' Forbus added tonelessly.

Dayna stopped breathing. 'Leitz?'

'Almost as vile a sadist as Sleer.' The clawlike hands squirmed and trembled, and the voice became a strident rasp. 'Yes, I should like Leitz to be here.' He noticed their sudden stillness, and said, 'Is something wrong?'

Dayna bit her lip. 'Leitz told us he worked for the resistance.'

Tarrant looked at her. 'But he didn't tell us about the booby-trapped door, did he?'

Dayna stared back at him. 'He must have set Hunda up too,' she realised. 'That story about the monorail tunnel—it's a trap!'

'We must find Hunda and warn him.' Tarrant turned to the man in the wheelchair and said urgently, 'Forbus, we came here to get a sample of Pylene-50 in the hope that somebody can devise a protection against——'

Forbus held up his clawlike hand. 'Somebody already has, Tarrant.' He pushed himself across to a store cupboard and took out a clear plastic vial filled with tiny green capsules. 'These block the effects of Pylene-50, though unfortunately they do not reverse them. Here.' He handed the vial to Tarrant and reached to the back of the cupboard for an envelope. 'And this is the chemical formula. Take it.'

'Forbus,' Dayna said, struggling to express herself. 'We want you to——'

'Don't waste time thanking me, my friends.' Forbus shooed them away. 'You must hurry. Hurry!'

One hand pressed to his headset, the duty tracer half turned in his seat and said, 'Flight Commander requests clearance to launch, sir.'

'Yes, go ahead,' said Colonel Quute, standing next to his desk.

'Strike Leader, this is Magnetrix Missile Control. You have clearance.'

The General strode into the room and Quute came forward, tugging his tunic straight. 'Just launching the search for that spy-ship, sir.'

'Good. What's the position regarding the monorail?'

'The sapper team has laid eighteen charges in the tunnel. They can be detonated independently or simultaneously.'

The General looked at Quute. 'I suppose Leitz will expect a medal after this,' he said testily, and struck himself quite hard on the thigh with his silver-capped baton.

On board *Scorpio* the computer reported: 'Surface launch, Master.'

Vila bounded off the crash-couch. 'What did I tell you.'

At the flight control module Avon had his eyes fixed on the three blips in the lower left quadrant of the scanner. Alongside him in the co-pilot's position, Soolin leaned forward tensely.

'Can you identify, Slave?' Avon asked.

'The heat pattern indicates three B19 cruisers.'

'Oh, come on, Avon,' Vila implored, hopping up and down. 'Hit that button!'

'That's a search formation, Avon,' Soolin said, glancing at him. 'They're not lined for an attack.'

'So they're searching!' Vila yelped. He looked frantically from one to the other. 'Are we going to wait till they find us? Let's get out!'

'They must have picked up Tarrant and Dayna and

realised we're up here somewhere.' Avon looked up from the scanner, his nostrils white and pinched. While his crewmembers were still down there he was reluctant to move out of teleport range, but he had no choice. He flexed his fist and rapped out, 'Slave, set the ship on an evasion pattern at maximum speed.'

Vila rolled his eyes in relief. 'That's the first sensible——'

'Just a minute!' Soolin pointed to the light flashing on the communication console. She flicked the channel open. 'This is *Scorpio*. Come in, Tarrant!'

'Hold that order, Slave,' Avon commanded.

Tarrant came through loud and clear. 'Soolin, we're almost finished here.'

'Tell him if he doesn't get the lead out we're certainly finished here!' Vila moaned, wringing his hands.

'Tarrant, we think *Scorpio*'s been spotted,' Soolin told him. 'Teleport up now!'

'Sorry, Soolin, we still have a couple of things to attend to.'

'Tarrant, listen to me!' Avon snarled. His eyes narrowed as the communicator light stopped flashing. 'Tarrant! Tarrant, you big dumb——'

'It's no use,' Soolin said, shaking her head. 'He's cut off.'

'Well, that-is-it!' Vila lifted both arms and gestured towards the scanner. 'With those ships out there we can't wait a second longer.'

'Maybe they aren't looking for us,' Soolin ventured.

'Are you crazy? You said yourself that's a search formation.'

The blonde girl shrugged. 'They haven't picked up Tarrant and Dayna, so why have they assumed there's a ship out here?' she wanted to know.

The same thought had occurred to Avon. He had an idea. 'Orac, that technical information you obtained from Space Centre. How was it relayed here?'

'Through Terminal four-zero-six,' the machine replied promptly.

Avon passed a hand across his eyes.

'The Terminal on Helotrix . . .'

'Of course,' said Orac promptly. 'The nearest Terminal to our present position.'

'That's how they did it,' Avon told the others wearily. 'They must have intercepted the transmission.'

'Computer logic.' Soolin smiled faintly and shook her head. 'The nearest Terminal.'

Vila glowered up at them. 'So Orac's thick. We all know that. Let's move!'

Avon came to a decision. 'I'm going in under them,' he said curtly, studying the screen.

'W-h-a-t?' Vila couldn't believe his ears.

'We'll go down to cloud level. If we're between them and the planet we won't show on their scanners.'

'But once we get below them we'll be cut off!' Vila shrieked. 'We won't stand a chance!'

'Give me manual control, Slave.' Avon gripped the twin control columns in readiness. 'I'm banking on them searching outwards, not inwards.'

'And if you're wrong?'

Avon spared him a brief, hooded glance. 'You can say I told you so. Providing you speak loudly and very fast,' he said, settling back in his seat.

Vaporous streamers of dawn mist lay close to the pock-marked ground and collected in grey pools in the shell-holes and craters. Like a stage-set, the ruined landscape was gradually illuminated and came to life as the fat distended sun appeared above the broken horizon.

With the growing light, figures could be seen moving carefully among the ruins. They advanced silently, using whatever cover offered itself. Ahead of them, a wall breached in several places marked the end of no-man's-land; beyond it lay the environs of the Magnetrix Terminal, swept by enemy detectors and firepower.

Hunda called a hurried conference of his section leaders.

The rest of the column melted out of sight, awaiting his signal.

'The entrance to the old monorail must be somewhere in this area,' he told them. 'Probably covered in rubble.'

Avandir peered through the thinning mist. 'It should be this side of the wall – near where the Armoury used to stand.'

The three men surveyed the desolation, trying to relate it to what they remembered. Suddenly Hask grabbed the Major's arm.

'Hunda – someone over there!'

They ducked down, unslinging their weapons. Two figures were clambering over the brow of a hill. Hask sighted along the barrel, and Hunda said, 'Hold it! I know them. Stay here.'

He picked his way towards Tarrant and Dayna and a few moments later all three returned. Hunda said, 'The raid's off.'

'Why?' Hask frowned, standing up.

'We've been tricked. Leitz is a double-agent.'

Tarrant said grimly, 'If you go into that monorail tunnel you're as good as dead. Your only chance is to go in the way we came out.'

'We'd be picked off before we got anywhere near the Terminal,' Avandir said dully.

'Hunda, if you issue your men with these you'll have a fighting chance,' Dayna said, holding up the vial.

'What are they?'

'Some new drug that counters the effect of their medical lasers,' Tarrant explained. 'It could give your men immunity.'

Hunda took the vial and looked at the tiny green capsules, his lined face brooding and thoughtful.

Colonel Quute and the General stood at the duty tracer's shoulder, watching the gridded screen with rapt attention. The attack was supposed to have taken place at dawn, half an hour ago, but as yet there had been no indication of it.

Quute was restive. He pushed a hand through his close-cropped hair and said, 'They should have entered the tunnel by now.'

'When they do we'll let them get well in and then blow every charge,' the General said, rocking slowly to and fro. 'Make it as quick as possible for the poor devils.'

A blip winked on.

'We have an entry signal, sir! Vector 4-K.'

Quute leaned forward. Vector 4-K? That couldn't be right. It was nowhere near the old monorail entrance. In fact it was damn near the——

'Must be a feint to draw attention from their main attack,' the General conjectured.

The blip divided into two, and then three.

Quute said worriedly, 'They look to be coming through in some strength, sir, for a feint.' He smacked his hands together. 'They've broached the Terminal perimeter!'

'They're moving towards the central concourse, sir,' the duty tracer confirmed.

'We'll have to cut them off,' the General decided. 'Tell Commissioner Sleer we need a troop of guards at Vector 4-K immediately.' He turned and headed for the door. 'I want to see this. Coming, Quute?'

'What about the tunnel?'

'What?' The General nodded briskly. 'Oh, yes. Detonate the charges now.'

He strode out, with a perturbed Colonel Quute at his heels.

Leading his column into the attack, Hunda felt the ground shake. There came a thunderous rumbling from deep underground, which made the shells of the buildings totter and brought masonry crashing down. Slowly the sounds of the explosion died away.

'You were right, Tarrant,' Hunda said, wiping the dust from his eyes. 'That was the monorail going up. Let's move!'

Advancing in line abreast, the column moved purposefully

towards the concourse, the only remaining obstacle between them and the Magnetrix Missile Control H.Q.

They were less than thirty yards away, seemingly without opposition, when they were caught in a concentrated crossfire of lasers, lancing in from all directions. So quick and unexpected, there wasn't time to retaliate. The column stumbled on for a few paces and then stood aimlessly, their weapons pointing at the ground. From out of the ruined buildings, medical lasers levelled, came the black-visored Federation troopers, and amongst them the slender black leather-clad figure of Commissioner Sleer.

Some little distance away, the General and Colonel Quute saw the Commissioner leap onto a hunk of concrete and stand arrogantly with feet apart, hands on hips. They heard the sharp command ring out:

'Put down your weapons!'

Dayna was staring at Commissioner Sleer as if she'd seen a ghost. Which wasn't far from the truth.

When at last she spoke it was in a hoarse, incredulous whisper.

'Servalan . . . !'

The sinister black figure whirled round. It was Servalan all right. No mistaking that sleek head and those haughty, glacial features. Nor that sneer of mocking triumph when she recognised two of her old, deadly enemies. And she had them at her mercy! Stunned into docile obedience along with the rest of these mangy Helot dogs!

Hunda had waited until all the troopers were in plain view. Pretending to lay his weapon on the ground, he glanced along the column, and then, with a savage, '*Now!*' straightened up firing from the hip.

The crack of carbine fire boomed and echoed deafeningly across the wasteland of rubble. Taken totally by surprise, the troopers were cut to pieces where they stood, the useless medical lasers clattering down as hands clutched chests and stomachs.

Side by side, the General and Colonel Quute reached for

their handguns. A shot took Quute in the throat, ripping it open like ripe fruit, and he was dead before he hit the ground. The General got his gun free just as a Helot leapt upon him. The light of battle was in the old warrior's eyes. 'Wonderful fighters at close . . .' he staggered back, coughing blood '. . . quarters.'

In all the confusion Tarrant had lost sight of Servalan. Then, through the smoke, Dayna glimpsed the slim black figure diving for cover behind a half-destroyed building, and pointed.

'After her!' Tarrant shouted.

By the time they'd reached the spot the area was deserted, a confusing intersection of narrow bombed streets branching away. They looked round helplessly. It would take a hundred men to comb them thoroughly.

Tarrant shook his head, breathing hard. 'She's given us the slip, Dayna.'

'It *was* Servalan, wasn't it?' Dayna said uncertainly.

Tarrant had no doubts. 'We both saw her. And she recognised us, too.' He raised his head as, distantly, they heard the sound of firing from the Missile Control HQ. Hunda and his column would storm through now, with nothing to stop them.

Dayna holstered her handgun and smiled at him inquiringly. Tarrant grinned back and spoke into his communicator. 'Tarrant to *Scorpio*. We're ready to teleport.'

On the flight deck, Vila's comment was terse and heartfelt. 'About time.'

Avon gestured towards Soolin, seated at the control console. 'Stand by to operate teleport. Where are those cruisers now, Slave?'

'Beyond range, Master. You outmanoeuvred them with consummate skill.'

'Set a direct course for base. Maximum speed.'

'Teleport operating,' Soolin called out.

A blue haze shimmered in the teleport bay and resolved itself into the shapes of Dayna and a still grinning Tarrant.

'What are you smirking about?' Vila asked indignantly, striding forward. 'Do you realise we've got half the Federation battle fleet looking for us?'

Avon was equally blunt. 'Next time either of you pull a stunt like that I promise you it'll be fatal. If I have to kill you myself.'

They stepped down from the teleport bay, and Dayna said, 'We've just seen an old friend of yours, Avon.'

'An implacable old friend,' Tarrant added.

Dayna was enjoying Avon's puzzled expression. She let him stew for a second or two, and then said with a crooked smile, 'Servalan!'

'Servalan?' Soolin frowned. 'I thought you said she was dead?'

'We did,' said Tarrant, unbuckling his ammunition belt.

'But she's not,' said Dayna. 'She's very much alive.'

Tarrant stood before the flight control module, looking up at Avon. 'How do you suppose she got off the *Liberator?*'

'Are you sure she did?'

Tarrant nodded gravely. 'It was Servalan all right.'

'I hope so,' Avon said, riveting all eyes upon him. 'I didn't want her to die like that. I wanted to kill her myself.'

His face was stiff, unyielding.

Chapter Twelve

The object of Avon's inexorable hatred was at that precise moment filled with hatred herself.

'You tricked me, Forbus!' she spat at the hunched figure in the wheelchair, standing over him in the laboratory, eyes blazing.

'No, Sleer,' the scientist protested in his piping voice. 'I assure you——'

'You did something to that last batch of Pylene-50,' she accused him.

'I did nothing!' Forbus glanced out of the corner of his eye at the black device with the single red button, tantalisingly just out of reach. 'Nothing at all, I assure you.' He edged his chair nearer the bench. 'Let me show you the test sample——'

'I'm going to cut off your drug for three days,' she told him with cold satisfaction. 'That means you'll die about another ten per cent, Forbus.'

'Please, don't do that!' he begged. 'Look, this is the sample here——'

His thin crabbed hand reached out and Servalan stepped forward and snapped icily. 'I'm going to teach you to obey me, Forbus, if I have to destroy all your skinny little body . . .'

She was staring at the device on the bench. A tiny pulse began to throb in her temple. Forbus made a despairing lunge for the red button. With a savage thrust of her booted foot, Servalan sent the wheelchair spinning across the laboratory. Knowing it was his last hope, Forbus gripped the wheels with his frail hands and used every ounce of his failing strength to reach the electrical contact in a final desperate bid.

He never made it. Quite coolly, Servalan slipped her handgun from its holster and fired point-blank. Forbus jerked and uttered a pathetic little cry, like that of a dying bird, and the wheelchair went over backwards, spilling the tiny wasted body onto the floor. It lay there, the life ebbing out of it in a spreading pool of blood.

'If you need a witness, Commissioner, I can swear it was self-defence,' said a soft voice. Leitz stepped forward, the widow's peak a sharp black vee under the glare of light.

'What are you doing here?' Servalan asked suspiciously.

'I followed you from the concourse,' Leitz said easily. 'Those two off-worlders were very anxious to find you,

Commissioner.' He smiled with his half-mocking eyes. 'They seemed to think they recognised you.'

'Really?'

'And of course Practor recognised you too, didn't he?' The smile stiffened, the eyes went hard. 'That's why you killed him.'

'What do you want, Leitz?' asked Servalan, icy calm.

'The Presidency.' Leitz pressed the palms of his hands together and gave half a shrug. 'Well, somebody has to take Practor's place. You could use your influence, I'm sure. And of course you'd know that your secret would be safe with me . . . Servalan.'

'I'm sure it would.' Servalan smiled, but it was to herself. 'However, I don't submit to blackmail,' she said blandly.

'There's always a first time . . . and it's better than being executed,' Leitz pointed out. 'After all, how many people have you killed to conceal your secret?'

He took her in his arms, and raised his eyebrows as she kissed him. They remained frozen there, like two black brushmarks, registering surprise, disbelief, and a growing sense of shock as she stabbed him in the back of the neck.

'Twenty-six now,' said Servalan. She stepped over the body and strode from the laboratory without a backward glance.

PART THREE
STARDRIVE

Chapter Thirteen

The huge jagged mass of the asteroid loomed out of the brilliant starfield. Formed aeons ago from the remnants of a supernova, composed of nickel-quartz and frozen methane, it tumbled slowly like a spiked battering-ram on an elliptical orbit round the Altern planetary system. Across its pitted and scarred surface lay the scattered wreckage of a spacecraft. A grim reminder that whenever an irrepressible force met an unstoppable object, the asteroid always came off best.

Which was precisely what seemed to be worrying everyone sick on board *Scorpio* – except Avon.

'That's it?' asked Soolin in alarm, watching the scanner.

Seated alongside Tarrant in the co-pilot's position, Avon nodded. 'Our passport into the Altern system and out again when we're finished,' he said crisply. 'Right under the noses of the Federation.'

'What's the mass of that thing?' asked Dayna, dry-mouthed.

'About two billion tons, I'd say.'

'Range one hundred thousand and closing,' rapped Tarrant, not daring to take his eyes off the instrument panel for an instant.

'Then I say the whole scheme's crazy,' Dayna muttered.

Vila swallowed. 'Two billion tons . . .'

'Training manual rule one: never fool with asteroids,' Tarrant said. 'They're what Murphy's Law is all about.'

'Murphy's Law?' Soolin asked. She discovered her right hand was numb from gripping the padded backrest of Tarrant's chair.

'Anything that can go wrong will go wrong,' Dayna replied hollowly.

'The crews of any Federation patrols will have been taught the same lesson, Tarrant,' Avon reminded him. 'At the same school.'

'You think that makes me feel any better?' Tarrant said. 'Range ninety thousand, converging velocity Standard by One.'

A warning light came on accompanied by a shrill alarm. Avon cancelled them on the panel, still watching the scanner. The asteroid was now taking up most of the screen, blocking out the stars.

Slave broke in hesitantly, 'I don't wish to speak out of turn, but we're on a direct collision course with a large——'

'We know,' Avon said shortly.

'I'm sorry, Master,' the computer persisted, 'but this body is——'

'Don't be sorry, just be quiet,' Avon snapped. He glanced round at the others and met the apprehensive, accusing stares of Dayna, Soolin and Vila. From the tense concentration of Tarrant's profile he knew they were all against him – including the damn computer.

Avon thumped the panel with his fist. 'If we want this heap of ironmongery to remain operational then we have to visit Altern 5 to recover Selsium ore to make fuel crystals.' His arm jerked out, pointing at the scanner screen. 'Hitching a ride into the Altern system on that asteroid is the only way we're going to get past the Federation patrols and within teleport range of the planet. Now——' his mouth thinned and his eyes sparkled dangerously, '——if anyone's got a better idea, let's hear it.'

'I wish I'd kept my mouth shut,' Vila mumbled to no one in particular.

'Range sixty thousand.'

'Well,' Soolin said sardonically, 'if it worked for one of Vila's raids during his space piracy days . . .'

Vila wouldn't meet her look. 'I wasn't actually there in person when it was done, of course,' he admitted, a touch uncomfortably.

'You do surprise me,' the blonde girl retorted.

'The theory's sound enough,' said Avon impatiently, and turned back to the screen as Tarrant called out:

'Range fifty thousand. Maybe we should start planning just how to put theory into practice before that thing flattens us,' the curly-headed pilot suggested wryly.

Nearer now, on a head-on collision course, it was possible to gain a real idea of the size of the massive, slowly tumbling hunk of jagged rock and frozen methane. And the idea was terrifying. The huge asteroid dwarfed the ship in the same ratio as a melon to a pea; the slightest miscalculation and they would be splattered across it like a fly on a windscreen.

Avon ordered everyone to strap down tight. Vila and the two girls took to the crash-couches, and could do nothing except watch, listen and wait while Tarrant, Avon and *Scorpio*'s guidance systems worked in close co-ordination to perform the delicate fingertip manouevres that would make all the difference between survival and crunching oblivion in deep space.

Tarrant punched the latest readouts into the computer and requested an update, to which Slave replied:

'Thirty seconds thrust at maximum power vectored at three-point-nine-seven will match our course and velocity through the Altern system with the asteroid.'

'Thrust vectors set,' Tarrant said, adjusting a calibrated dial. 'Stand by on over-ride monitor.'

Avon positioned his hand over the control key. 'Standing by.'

Staring at the curved bulkhead above, Soolin asked huskily, 'Just how close are you planning to get to that thing, Avon?'

'Fifty metres. Near enough to be inside its radar shadow without the risk of being damaged by its spin. Slave – bring close encounter guidance systems on-line for the final approach.'

'Yes, Master. Guidance systems on-line and standing by. Main drive thrust condition at green for activation on your command.'

Vila strained round to see, his eyeballs protruding like organ stops. 'Do we have to go that near? That spin won't just damage us if we overshoot; it'll rip the ship in half.'

Tarrant shot a worried glance at Avon. 'Vila's right. We need a safer stand-off distance.'

But Avon wasn't prepared to compromise. 'The closer we get, the less risk there is of being detected by a patrol.'

'There won't be anything left of us to detect unless we match velocity and speed right now,' Dayna prophesied, watching the asteroid which now completely filled the screen.

'Range five thousand,' Tarrant chanted.

'Thirty seconds,' Avon alerted everyone. 'Stand by!'

Tarrant blinked his eyes to clear the sweat away. 'We can't risk leaving it that long,' he said hoarsely. 'Maximum thrust will wreck the main drive——'

He reached out to the throttle control and Avon grabbed his wrist.

'Listen, Tarrant, we can't risk a patrol detecting plasma radiation from a sustained thrust. We *have* to go for maximum.' The corner of his mouth curved sardonically but his eyes were hard and bright. 'There are times when even confirmed cynics must trust to luck.'

The asteroid was almost upon them, massive, menacing, relentless, bearing down with colossal momentum.

The final seconds ticked away.

Avon was poised over the instrument panel, his lips miming numbers. At last he gave the order – 'Now!' – and Tarrant opened the main drive to full thrust.

The ship surged forward, straining to keep the precious few metres between itself and the asteroid. And it was succeeding. They were maintaining a safe trajectory. Until a systems circuit overloaded and blew itself up in a shower of sparks right under Tarrant's nose. Coughing as the blue vapour bit the back of this throat, Tarrant yelled, 'Precision guidance lost!'

'Slave!' Avon shouted. 'Initiate the back-up system!'

There was a short, pregnant pause and then the voice explained apologetically, 'I'm very sorry about this, but that *was* the back-up system.'

The next moment was turmoil as the ship staggered under a tremendous shuddering blow. It canted steeply, throwing everyone hard against the restraining straps. The lighting flickered and dimmed and then went out altogether, leaving the flight deck bathed in the eerie red glow of the emergency globes.

Swinging away from the point of impact, a deep gash in its main drive tube, the ship hung above the jagged surface of rock and ice, snared within the ambience of the asteroid's mass and momentum as it swept on its trajectory through the Altern system.

It took the crew several moments to regain their orientation and to realise they were still alive and, though badly shaken, unharmed.

'Slave, damage reports,' Avon requested, checking the instrumentation.

'Main drive lost——'

'We know that. What about the outer hull?'

'No external or internal sensors are functioning in the plasma chamber or the main thrust tube, therefore damage to the ship's stern must be considerable. I'm sorry, Master.'

'*He's* sorry?' Soolin murmured, folding her arms.

'The chances are we've wrecked the main drive's focusing coil,' Tarrant guessed.

'We carry a spare,' Vila chirped up hopefully.

'And what use will that be?' Tarrant asked scathingly. 'The main drive chamber can't be pressurised. How do you carry out a sophisticated repair operation wearing a spacesuit and size ten gauntlets?'

'It's impossible,' said Dayna, unfastening the straps and sliding cautiously off the couch. She looked across at Avon in the dim red light. 'Like using an asteroid as cover to sneak into the Altern system. Maybe next time you'll listen to reason. If there is a next time. Which seems unlikely.'

115

'Slave, what's our life-support capability?' Avon inquired.

'One hundred and fifty-five hours and twenty-nine minutes, Master.'

Soolin rose from the couch, stretching her lithe body. 'By the time the oxygen runs out we'll be bored as well as dead,' she remarked sourly.

Avon wasn't one for giving in so easily. 'Let's run a full check on all systems,' he ordered. 'I'd prefer to be sure that dying's the best option we have left.'

Trapped in the gravitational embrace of a giant asteroid, without power and limited oxygen, it looked as if their options had dwindled to precisely that.

The lighting had been restored to normal, which made the scene on the flight deck only marginally more cheerful.

It was small consolation when set against the inescapable fact that without the main drive unit they were doomed to circle endlessly, helpless prisoners of the slowly tumbling asteroid. Endlessly in this case having the exact limitation of one hundred and forty-eight hours and seventeen minutes.

Slumped in the co-pilot's chair, Avon gazed dully at the blank screen. The rest of the crew, conscious of the need to conserve oxygen, lay sprawled on the crash-couches. Speculation had been exhausted hours ago, and with it, their last lingering hopes. Only Vila seemed to have found a fresh source of hope and comfort – in the shape of a small silver flask which he now turned upside down, peering into it with a glazed, screwed-up eye.

When nothing came out, he lurched to his feet and moved unsteadily across the flight deck, grinning amiably at his morose companions.

'. . . Hi there, everyone. Anyone for a party? You'll have to bring your own booze 'cos I've drunk mine . . .' He shook the upended flask in the air. 'Anyone got any booze?' he asked brightly. Oblivious to the lack of response, Vila fixed his wavering eyes on the slim blonde girl and leaned heavily against her, draping an arm across her shoulders.

'And how about my little cold, calculating Soolin?' he mumbled hazily. 'I'd like to see you unbend just a little bit before we're all . . . all . . . ' He belched, waving the flask about.

With an expression of distaste, Soolin squirmed away. Dayna said coldly, 'Sometimes you can be quite disgusting.'

Vila's eyebrows shot up in befuddled outrage. He staggered across to her and flopped down on the next couch, suddenly getting a fit of giggles. 'Not so, my lovely. I can be disgusting *all* the time. S'easy . . . ' He beamed mischievously across the flight deck. 'S'easy as colliding with an asteroid, eh, Avon?'

Vila leaned up on one elbow, his expression suddenly mournful. 'Know what they say 'bout your life passing before you when you're 'bout to . . . you know . . . ' He gave the thumbs-down sign. 'S'what's happening to me now,' he said tearfully. 'All my past life . . . ' He swept his hand in front of him as if to indicate a vast panorama.

'That's one misfortune we don't have to share,' said Avon gratefully.

Vila sighed. 'Fourteen I was when I was first sent to a penal colony. Ship was hit in the main drive by a meteoroid. Bang! Know what they did to repair it? Activated the force wall and generated an atmosphere outside the hull so that a repair gang could work in a vacuum without spacesuits. 'Cos it wasn't a vacuum any more, if you see what I mean . . . '

Avon turned his head to look at Vila for the first time. Then he looked at Tarrant, who had sat up.

'. . . clever those old prison hulk skippers,' Vila burbled, smiling fondly at the memory.

'Slave!' Avon was leaning forward, his face keenly alert. 'Activate the force wall and pressurise it with our air reserves!'

'That would be most inadvisable, Master,' the computer warned meekly. 'I'm terribly sorry, but our force wall generator is in extremely poor condition.'

Tarrant got to his feet. 'Slave's right, Avon. We'd lose the lot.'

Slave said tentatively, 'The best I could manage would be a blister force wall around the damaged part of the hull.'

'Do it!' Avon snapped. He climbed out from behind the flight control module, gestured to Tarrant, and the two men went through into the main hold section.

Soolin watched them leave and shook her head bemusedly at Vila. 'Out of the mouths of drunks and——'

'Drunk?' Vila sat up, his eyes wide, steady, unblinking. He said gently, 'Who's drunk?'

'You are,' Dayna said uncertainly.

Vila smiled and held up the flask. 'Tell me how to get drunk on plain water and I won't waste time.'

'Then why pretend?'

'Because, my lovely, no one ever tells someone who's drunk to volunteer. I don't like working in main drive chambers – especially main drive chambers that are isolated from space by one of Slave's force walls.'

Vila wasn't the fool he looked, Dayna thought. But then he couldn't be.

Crouching in the confined space between the main thrust unit and the seared black curvature of the drive chamber, Tarrant unslung the replacement plasma coil from his shoulder and set it down carefully. Avon sidled in behind him carrying a heavy multi-layered tool-kit. Each layer opened independently, giving access to any of the compartments.

The drive chamber itself was about twenty feet in length. At the business end, near the discharge tube, the last half-dozen helical turns of the plasma focusing coil were burnt and severely distorted. Adjacent to it, the drive chamber wall had been punctured, and through the gaping hole they could see where the outer hull had been ripped open by the impact.

Bright, diamond-hard stars gilded everything with a faint, icy sheen; it was difficult to believe that they were separated from the sub-zero vacuum of space by just a few cubic feet of pressurised air, held precariously in position by a blister force wall.

Tarrant, for one, preferred not to think about it. After inspecting the damage, he reported to the flight deck over his throat mike. 'We're in the main drive chamber. It's going to take about an hour, as near as we can tell.'

'Okay,' Soolin answered over the headset. 'We'll stay on watch.'

'See if you can sober up Vila,' said Tarrant, glancing at Avon.

'We'll try.'

Tarrant could have sworn there was a smile in her voice, though through the distortion it was hard to be sure. He squatted down beside Avon, who had opened the tool-kit and was taking out a number of plastic metal regenerator packs. When placed round the site of the damaged hull, and activated by microwave, these would form a smooth heat-resistant shell, sealing the hole effectively until a more permanent repair job could be carried out in dock.

The young pilot felt the hairs prickle on his spine. 'This is weird – like being in space without a spacesuit.'

Avon grunted, intent on positioning the regenerator packs. He reached down and took the control unit from the top compartment, raised the antennae, and switched on. The unit hummed. After a moment or two the packs began to lose their shape and spread. Avon attached the control unit by its magnetic base to the inner hull. 'Regeneration should take about thirty minutes.' He leaned back in the cramped space. 'While we deal with the coil.'

Twenty minutes later they had removed the burnt section of coil and fitted its replacement. The most critical part of the operation was yet to come: attaching the circuits in the correct sequence to a digital-coded junction panel. For this, Tarrant selected one of the glowing fibre-optic terminals, holding it delicately in a pair of padded tweezers, and passed it to Avon, who fed it into the appropriate hole in the panel, then clamped it fast.

There were more than fifty terminals altogether, and they

still had ten to connect when they were interrupted in their complex task by Soolin, her voice thin with urgency.

'Avon, Tarrant – we've got company. Three ships, possibly interceptors, range two hundred thousand, closing fast.'

Concentrating on threading and clamping a terminal, Avon said over the throat mike, 'Have they detected us?'

On the flight deck, Dayna leaned over the communication console, her eyes following the three speeding craft on the screen. 'It doesn't look like it. They're not on an intercept course.'

'What class are they?'

The three crew members frowned at one another. Soolin said, 'That's just it. None of us are sure.'

'But they've got a Federation look about them,' Vila added nervously.

'We can't leave what we're doing,' Avon said curtly. There was a slight pause, and he went on, 'Make a recording. We'll look at it later.'

Dayna pressed the tab. 'Hologram recorder rolling. Slave, keep the sensors zeroed on those ships.'

The regenerator packs had now formed and hardened, sealing the outer hull. Tarrant passed another of the glowing terminals to Avon. Only three more to go, he noted thankfully. He tried to ease his long legs in the cramped drive chamber and felt a stab of pins and needles in his thighs.

Avon held out his tweezers for the next terminal and the entire chamber was suddenly flooded with an intense, blinding light. The two men recoiled and instinctively shielded their eyes.

'Dayna, what's happening?' Avon cried out.

'Those three ships . . . they just exploded.'

'They *what*?' Tarrant said incredulously.

'I know it sounds crazy, but they just blew up by themselves,' the girl told them, sounding as baffled as they were.

Completing the last three connections hurriedly, Avon carried out a final check and closed the junction panel.

'Should get us back to base, anyway,' Tarrant said.

They collected their gear together and edged back along the drive chamber. Tarrant was right, Avon reflected. The replacement coil and patched-up hull would get them back to Xenon safely. But the main drive unit itself was antiquated and lacked the power they needed. In its present condition, *Scorpio* was a sitting duck for Federation interceptors and pursuit ships. Somehow or other they were going to have to soup it up – if they wanted to survive.

And that was the name of the game. Survival.

Chapter Fourteen

The darkened Crew Room at Xenon base flickered with the images on the large vis-screen. Three sleek black craft in tight formation zooming in against a backdrop of blurred stars. An eye-blink later there were three fireballs and flaming debris spinning off into space. And after that, a haze of vaporised particles which gradually faded away to nothing: instantaneous, inexplicable annihilation.

Dayna pressed a key to clear the screen and turned on the lights. Nobody spoke. Because nobody had a clue about how three ships could destruct for no apparent reason.

'A most fascinating recording,' observed Orac succinctly.

'We're looking for conclusions, not critical acclaim,' Avon remarked tartly.

'Very well.' Orac hummed softly to himself. 'Two conclusions. First: the Federation have re-established their ship-building programme ahead of my prediction. Second: the crude design of the main drives indicates that they have lost their top designer.'

'Orac,' Tarrant said wearily, 'we had worked that out already. What we want to know is how three ships can suddenly blow up by themselves——'

'If that is what happened I should want an answer to the same question,' Orac replied cryptically.

Tarrant sighed and looked round at the others. For a supposedly super-brain, Orac could be maddeningly non-communicative.

Avon rose from the couch and regarded Orac thoughtfully. 'So what you're trying to tell us is that those ships *didn't* blow up by themselves.'

'I'm not *trying* to tell you anything,' Orac replied waspishly. 'I am simply not interested in attempting to compensate for your amazing lack of observation.'

Avon stroked his chin. He glanced shrewdly towards Dayna. 'Run the recording again – this time at half-speed,' he ordered.

Dayna keyed up the images and everyone watched a re-run of the three ships exploding in slow-motion. When it was over, and as much at a loss as ever, Vila piped up truculently, 'So what was that supposed to tell us?'

'That recording told Orac something,' Avon said, nodding, 'and the only way to find out what it was is to check every frame.'

Dayna groaned. 'At ten thousand frames per second? It'll take hours.'

Avon strode out. 'We'll transfer it to the Ops Room and take it in shifts,' he said, indifferent to the pained looks passing amongst the others. He didn't like mysteries; and besides, he had a hunch about this one.

It was Dayna who found it.

An hour into the third shift she was sitting, getting very bored, watching the monitor screen in the Operations Room, taking in each separate frame of the hologram recording, when something that shouldn't have been there suddenly was. Had she been yawning at the time she might have missed it – for the tiny, stubby-finned spacecraft appeared on only three frames – and on only one of them was there a complete image.

No wonder they hadn't spotted it before, even at half-speed. To have passed through the hologram scan in three frames, when the recorder was running at ten thousand frames a second, meant that the ship was travelling at an incredible rate. Dayna couldn't conceive how fast – but it was shifting like a bat out of hell and no mistake.

At once she called Avon and the others, who clustered round her chair as she replayed the same sequence, freezing the frame which contained the complete image. Even here the craft was slightly blurred on the trailing edges, some indication of its tremendous speed.

'About Standard by Twelve at a guess,' Tarrant hazarded.

'In real-time?' Vila squeaked disbelievingly. 'That's not possible!'

'Standard by Twelve decimal Six, to be precise,' Orac informed them.

'Nothing can travel at that speed in real-time,' Dayna protested. 'The *Liberator* was only capable of Standard by Ten flat out – and that was the most advanced spacecraft ever built.' She shook her dark cropped head. 'It's impossible.'

'Nothing "could" and "It was impossible",' Orac corrected her in his languid, superior voice. 'It is necessary for your statement to be rephrased using the past tense.'

Soolin studied the screen, her beautiful, flawless face set in a frown. 'So whatever it was, it fired three bolts at those ships before it passed in front of our sensors.'

'And at Standard by Twelve they never knew what hit them,' said Vila.

'Just as well it left us alone.' Soolin looked at the others. 'So what is it?' she inquired.

Tarrant said, 'A single-seater space chopper. They were a teenagers' craze a couple of centuries back until the Federation outlawed them.'

'Hardly surprising if they could do Standard by Twelve,' Dayna commented wryly.

'They couldn't,' Avon said with a brisk shake of the head.

'Which means that this one has been fitted with a new form of main drive unit.'

Orac took the speculation further. 'Which also means that the photonic spacedrive has been finally perfected by Dr Plaxton.'

'Who?' Vila asked, blinking.

'Plaxton was the head of the Federation's Spacedrive Research Centre,' Avon said. 'Go on, Orac.'

'At the time of the Federation's collapse the doctor was developing a new spacedrive system which used light instead of plasma to exert thrust. The Photonic Drive, or the Stardrive Machine, as it's known.'

Avon leaned against the bench and folded his arms. He narrowed his eyes thoughtfully and asked, 'Was the prototype small enough to be fitted into a space chopper?'

'Certainly.'

'Hey – just think!' Vila's face lit up. 'If we could get hold of one of those drives and swap it for the clapped-out unit in our ship . . .'

Avon had already considered that possibility. 'Where is this Dr Plaxton now?' he asked Orac.

'Presumably with the owners of that space chopper,' Orac replied testily, obviously displeased at having to state self-evident facts. 'It's all a matter of observation.'

Avon smiled to himself. Another of Orac's famous cryptic clues. Well then, if observation was the key . . . 'Can you bring that thing into close-up?' he asked Dayna, nodding at the screen.

The girl's slim dark fingers moved expertly over the slider controls and the image swelled until they were able to make out more detail. Smooth tapering body, about twelve feet from tip to stern. A pair of short stubby fins with plasma bolt projectors slung underneath. In the nose section, a single-piece blister through which they could see the silver-helmeted head of the pilot, his eyes hidden behind tinted goggles.

'Go in closer. Concentrate on the pilot.'

Further magnified, it was possible to make out the expression on his face, thick lips drawn back in a snarl of triumph. There was an emblem of some kind on his helmet. Avon leaned over Dayna's shoulder. 'Focus on the helmet.'

The emblem grew and resolved itself into a black rat with vicious teeth and claws, holding aloft a dagger dripping blood.

Vila gave an audible gasp.

'It's a Space Rat!'

Soolin arched an eyebrow. 'Friends of yours, Vila?'

'Friends! Space Rats!' Vila was staring at the screen with bulging eyes. 'There's no such thing as a friend of a Space Rat – they even hate each other.' He shuddered and shook himself, as if casting off a gruesome nightmare.

'What else do you know about them?' Tarrant asked him.

'They're maniacs – psychopaths. All they live for is sex and violence, tattoos and speed. And the fellers are just as bad. We had a couple on the penal colony once,' Vila recalled in a chilled voice. 'They were always trying to frighten me.'

'And they didn't succeed, of course,' said Dayna, pokerfaced. 'What were they imprisoned for?'

'Breaking into transport museums. When the Federation banned all leisure transport they went in for stealing anything that had wheels or could fly. They were all speed-crazy. And I do mean crazy!' Vila's fear and loathing were such that no one doubted him for a moment.

'Speed is the key,' Avon said, straightening up. He tapped his fist into his palm. 'Find the Space Rats and we find Plaxton.'

Vila backed away, raising his hands as if pushing back a tidal wave. 'Now look, Avon, I've tangled with just about every ugly in the book since I got involved with you lot – but I draw the line at Space Rats. Absolutely.'

Tarrant said, 'Orac, what do you know about Space Rats?'

'They are the sum total of human illogicality. They have no respect for authority or life. What culture they have is similar to an ancient Earth sect – the so-called Hell's Angels. There the similarity ends: Hell's Angels did have some standards, whereas the Space Rats have none.'

'Where can we find them?' Avon wanted to know.

'Their last known base was Caspar – an Earth-type planet in Sector Five.'

'Sector Five?' Soolin shook her head dubiously. 'We'd never make it with the state the ship's in.'

Dayna said, 'What are our chances, Orac?'

'One hundred per cent better than your chances of getting anywhere else if you don't obtain a new spacedrive for the ship within three months,' the machine answered with deadly logic.

'Thanks, Orac,' Dayna grimaced. 'That's a great help.'

There was a brief silence, everyone locked inside their own thoughts, silently weighing the odds. They weren't good, whichever way you looked at them.

Finally, Tarrant said, 'It's going to take some time to get the ship ready.'

'As ready as it ever can be,' Soolin said glumly.

'Well then.' Avon looked round, his face hard and purposeful. 'The sooner we get on with it, the better.'

And with that he led them from the room. All except Vila, who lingered behind, glaring at the Space Rat emblem on the screen. 'You know something, Orac?' he muttered with a mixture of outrage and disgust. 'There are times when your mouth is almost as big as mine.'

'Vila!' somebody shouted.

Vila raised his fists impotently to heaven. 'Yeah, yeah!' he croaked, stumping after them.

'Synchronous orbit round Caspar established.' Tarrant set the orbital co-ordinates and activated the auto-guidance system. 'And locked.'

From this point on the ship's systems would compensate automatically for any drift or divergence from the pre-set orbit.

Vila was on pins. Throughout the trip he'd made everyone's life a constant misery with his badgering, his sulks, his outbursts, and his baleful predictions of what might befall them. Now he was wearing Avon's patience down to a fine point with a barrage of nervous conjectures.

'Supposing they come at us with one of their space choppers?'

'There's no percentage in worrying about that,' Avon replied shortly.

'No? After what happened to those Federation ships?'

'Because we won't know anything about it.' Avon turned away. 'Try again, Soolin.'

At the communication console, Soolin touched a key and spoke into the button microphone. 'Caspar, Caspar. This is civilian freighter *Scorpio* calling Caspar. We are not hostile, repeat, not hostile. We wish to negotiate an alliance against the Federation. Caspar, Caspar. This is *Scorpio*. Do you copy?'

'You're wasting your time,' Vila jeered. 'They won't have radio. The only technology they're interested in is on wheels, or flies, or goes bang. You know——' He was about to give Avon the benefit of his opinion when Avon nodded to Tarrant, and the two crossed to the teleport control desk. So instead Vila transferred his attention to the girls. 'You know what they're up to right now?' he said, pointing downwards. 'Right now they're trying to make up their minds which piece of nastiness they're going to send up to zap us.' He nodded adamantly, eyes wide and round.

Dayna said, 'Surely they won't risk an attack without finding out what it is they're going to attack?'

Vila held up his finger. 'That's the logical way of thinking. But those psychopaths down there are Space Rats. Their philosophy is simple. If it moves – zap it.'

Without looking up, Avon said, 'As you know so much about their philosophy, you're the ideal person to teleport down to talk to them.' He sounded perfectly serious.

Vila glanced over both shoulders and then pointed to his chest. 'Me?'

'Get permission for us to land the ship,' said Tarrant, busy with some calculations.

'Dayna will go down too,' said Avon. 'Keep an eye on you.'

'Oh wonderful,' Dayna said, with a distinct lack of enthusiasm. 'Thanks a lot.'

Vila still wasn't sure he'd heard right. 'You don't seriously expect us to *talk* to them?' he said incredulously.

'Just check the place out,' Avon told him. 'Make sure we're right.'

He adjusted the calibrated controls on the teleport desk and keyed up a picture on the central scanner screen. Everyone stopped what they were doing to watch. It was an infra-red scan of a bleak stretch of terrain, crossed by a deep ravine. Superimposed over the image was a circle enclosing the fine hairlines of a graduated marker. A low pulsing tone increased in pitch as Avon moved the marker near the edge of the ravine.

'This is your best estimate, Slave?'

'Thermal wake surveillance indicates that this is the inhabited region. The area is criss-crossed with thermal wakes caused by some form of machines.' The computer added tentatively, 'I hope my conclusions are correct, Master.'

'What sort of machines?' Tarrant asked.

'I fear that is beyond my humble capacity.'

Avon followed the wavering line of the ravine northwards and the pulsing tone rose shrilly.

'You're not going to put us down bang in the middle of their hide-out?' Dayna said in alarm.

The marker moved further south and the tone died to a low pulse. 'Two miles away,' Avon said. 'The walk will sharpen your senses. Better get kitted up. We don't want to hang around here a second longer than we have to.'

Vila glowered at him and went to the armaments locker, still grousing. 'Set those teleport co-ordinates properly – not in the middle of a lake or anything.'

'The state the final guidance is in, you'll be lucky not to end up in space on a reciprocal heading,' Soolin informed him cheerfully.

If looks could kill, Vila's would have struck her dead on the spot.

Dayna peered over the boulder. She frowned and turned around in a complete circle. Now how was that possible? she wondered. They'd teleported together, on exactly the same co-ordinates, and she was here and Vila wasn't.

The terrain looked no better down here than it had on the scanner. Grey chalky soil, compacted by the sun and rain to a solid, slablike consistency. Nothing could grow in this stuff, not even lichen. It reminded her of a lunar landscape, inert, totally lifeless. Not the ideal place to spend a vacation. Not the ideal place for anything.

'Vila?' she called out softly. Even her voice sounded flat and dead in this bleak wilderness. 'Vila!'

A stone clattered down the shale-covered slope to her left. Dayna spun round, the handgun drawn and levelled in an instant. Her shoulders slumped and she holstered the weapon with a weary sigh.

'You really think this is the time for fooling about?' she inquired of Vila, lodged halfway up the slope, his foot wedged between two rocks. He looked down despairingly.

'I'm stuck,' he said plaintively.

'So am I, Vila,' Dayna muttered irritably. 'With you.'

She climbed up and helped him extricate himself. As he sat massaging his ankle, Dayna cocked her head. 'Listen!'

Distantly, they heard the throaty roar of engines. Scrambling higher, they flattened themselves on the damp chalky surface squinted cautiously over the rim of the rock-strewn hill.

'What do you think it is ?' Dayna asked.

'How should I know?'

The stuttering roar seemed to fade, and then it burst out deafeningly as two riders topped the next rise and raced towards them. Dayna and Vila dug their chins into the chalk. It really seemed as if the two gleaming machines were going to roar up the hill towards them, when at the very last moment the riders swung them hard about on a sliding swerve and braked to a halt about twenty yards away. With engines idling, they lifted their tinted goggles onto their silver helmets and removed their black leather gauntlets. One of them took a pair of binoculars from a side pannier and did a slow sweep of the surrounding countryside.

Dayna nudged Vila with her elbow. 'Are they . . . ?' she mouthed.

Vila nodded grimly, his face ashen. 'Space Rats.'

'What are they riding?'

Vila shrugged. 'If it moves on wheels, they steal it. If it moves without wheels, they zap it. They don't like complications.'

Dayna was beginning to share Vila's morbid fear of the Space Rat fraternity. If these two specimens were anything to go by, she wasn't looking forward to meeting any of the others. They were both squat, powerfully-built, with heavily-muscled arms and shoulders. Their riding gear was an odd mixture of patched leather and animal skins, decorated with bits of fur, and held together by zips, chains and thongs. They wore broad studded belts, at the waist and diagonally across their chests, and pearl-handled guns strapped to their bulky thighs.

But it was their expressions she liked least of all. Thick-lipped, slit-eyed, with flat noses and flaring nostrils, they had a gross swarthy ugliness that was verging on deformity. Even from here she thought she could smell stale sweat.

The recce complete, the two Space Rats adjusted their goggles, revved their machines to a howling crescendo, and shot away. Seconds later they were two racing black dots in the bare bleached landscape.

Vila sat up, wiping his mouth with a trembling hand. 'Seems like luck is on our side today,' he breathed.

'You think so?' Dayna murmured, staring past his head,

and when Vila jerked round he found himself looking directly into the shiny lens of a TV camera mounted on a rusty pedestal.

Chapter Fifteen

A worried face loomed forward and filled the screen. The man watching it lay sprawled on a heap of stained and evil-smelling cushions, one enormous booted leg crossed over the other. Around him were scattered, like broken toys abandoned by a spoilt, wilful child, bits and pieces of highly advanced technological hardware, most with their electronic innards dangling out.

The man stared at the screen with slitted eyes. The hairy hand holding the hunk of meat came up to the bearded mouth and there was the crunch of animal bone and wet chewing sounds followed by a deep belly-rippling belch. Stripped of its flesh, the splintered bone was tossed to the ground, to be set upon by four large black rats, who squealed and squabbled for what was left.

Another face, that of a young black girl, appeared alongside the first. She was very beautiful. The bearded man grunted, wiping his greasy fingers on the tangled black hair of his chest through the tattered fur cape fastened by a steel pin at his throat.

The worried face relaxed and looked relieved. 'It's all right. This thing's ancient. Chances are it hasn't been working for years.'

The girl nodded, though she didn't look convinced. The faces went.

Reaching out, the bearded man's thick fingers scoured the floor, a large ring with a rat clutching a bloody dagger glinting on his middle finger. He found the remote-control device and jabbed a button. The picture changed. Now it showed the man and the girl as tiny figures, moving towards the camera. In the bleak grey landscape they looked puny and vulnerable.

The bearded man settled back on the furs, picking at a shred of meat stuck between his square yellow teeth with a broken, dirt-rimmed fingernail.

Tarrant flicked a row of switches and activated the countdown. 'Descent from orbit begins in forty-five seconds and counting.'

The numerals ticked away on the central digital display.

Soolin paused in the act of buckling the straps on the crash-couch and gave Avon an accusing stare. 'You never intended to wait for Vila and Dayna to report back, did you? You're just using them.'

Avon leaned back in the co-pilot's chair. 'Vila and Dayna are a useful diversion,' he said indifferently.

'If they get caught.'

'Which is fairly likely,' Tarrant said, intent on the readouts in front of him.

'I wouldn't count too heavily on that.' Soolin gave the strap a final jerk and lay back, sweeping the tousled blonde hair from her eyes. 'Dayna's sharp and she handles a gun quite well considering her sheltered upbringing.'

Tarrant grinned lazily. 'Tune the detectors to the radio spectrum, Soolin, and you'll discover about fifty radiation sources dotted around that area.' He glanced across at her. 'Caused by leakage from badly maintained TV surveillance cameras.'

'That's in addition to the strong radiation source near their base,' Avon said. 'It's at the sort of level you'd expect from a high-energy research laboratory . . .'

'. . . or a test chamber for a new spacedrive,' Tarrant added, meeting Avon's eye.

The look wasn't lost on Soolin. She said bitterly, 'So you've let Dayna and Vila walk into a trap.'

'We need that spacedrive,' Avon said flatly, and gripped

the padded armrests as the ship lurched and the whine of the main drive unit began to build.

'Retro sequence running.' Tarrant adjusted his straps and moulded his fingers round the twin control columns. 'Cheer up, Soolin. Bringing this bag of bolts down through the atmosphere looks set to be a lot more dangerous than anything Dayna and Vila are likely to come across.'

'If that's any consolation,' Avon added.

'No,' Soolin said stiffly, staring fixedly at the bulkhead above her. 'It isn't.'

The area below the cliff-face resembled a junkyard. Hulks of rusting machinery and the gutted remains of surface vehicles and airborne craft were scattered about. There was an air of dereliction, for which the steep, fissured chalk face made a perfect backdrop.

Using the cover offered by a landslip of rocks, Dayna and Vila surveyed this machine graveyard with conflicting emotions. Dayna was suspicious and uneasy, while Vila couldn't hide a surge of eager relief.

'We've made a mistake,' he said happily. 'There's nothing here.'

Dayna sharpened the focus on the magni-viewer and did a slow scan from the rusting relics to the cliff-face. She became very still for a moment, then lowered the viewer, her expression thoughtful. 'They must hope that everyone thinks as you do – including the Federation.' She handed him the viewer. 'There's everything here if you look.'

Almost reluctantly, Vila did. He didn't want to see the three stone doorways blending into the cliff-face, nor the vehicle tracks leading out from them, but the evidence was there in front of his eyes, unmistakable, irrefutable.

He said dismally, 'Concealed entrances.'

'Right.' Dayna slipped the magni-viewer into its case. 'And it looks like they've got enough scrap here to build a small fleet of space choppers.'

'Well,' said Vila wanly, putting on the bravest face

he could manage, 'at least we've got the advantage of surprise.'

Above them, not ten feet away, hidden amongst the rocks, a TV camera peered down with its single beady eye.

Napier made a minute adjustment to the thermocouple and sat back on his heels. The air in the test chamber had the faint acrid tang of burnt ozone. The middle-aged scientist tried not to sneeze: after all this time he should be used to it, but maybe he'd developed an allergy. His nose twitched, he tried to stifle it, and sneezed, receiving an austere glare from Dr Plaxton above her rimless spectacles.

Napier looked abashed. Like her, he was garbed in a sterile coverall and wearing transparent surgical gloves. The photonic drive was Dr Plaxton's baby, and she cossetted it more than any mother her human offspring.

And particularly today of all days when the first full-scale test of the Mark II prototype was about to take place. This was an even more efficient version of the original spacedrive, to which Dr Plaxton had devoted all her energy and ingenuity for several years past. Even before she left the Federation Spacedrive Research Centre the idea had been germinating in her fertile brain. And now, against all odds, working alone and independently, she had achieved her ultimate dream.

It was a staggering scientific breakthrough – if it came up to the expectations raised by the trials on the Mark I.

'Particle drive control,' Dr Plaxton called out, reading from the checklist on the control panel in front of her. She glanced up sharply, her grey-streaked hair drawn back severely into a tight bun. 'You'd better double-check that, Napier. I'm going to take the drive up to seventy-five per cent output.'

'In here, doctor?'

The prematurely-balding man looked round apprehensively at the hewn limestone walls, which had been partially lined with soundproofing baffles. The photonic drive, under its clear plastic canopy, took up most of the available space; even the two Space Rats, assigned to help with manual tasks, were lounging somewhat uncomfortably amidst a jumble of test equipment. They had refused to wear sterile smocks, and still had on their usual tatty and dirty clothes, making them appear both incongruous and ridiculous. Like a couple of hairy apes in an operating theatre, Napier thought.

'Don't argue,' Dr Plaxton snapped, her mouth a thin straight line. 'I know what I'm doing.'

Napier bent once more to carry out the check, then reported meekly. 'Particle drive satisfactory, Dr Plaxton.'

'Good.' Dr Plaxton ticked off the final item on the checklist. 'Place the photon shield in position.'

Napier closed the access port in the canopy and rose to his feet, nodding to the two Space Rats, who straightened up indolently, making no attempt to disguise their utter boredom, and started to wheel the cumbersome lead-lined shield towards the thrust tube at the rear of the test bed.

'Stop!!'

They halted, their dull-witted faces confused, slitted eyes blinking in consternation.

'How many times must I tell you!' Dr Plaxton stormed across and thrust two pairs of surgical gloves under their broad, flat noses. 'You wear these in here! All the time – understand?'

'Look, lady, we're only movin' the bleedin' shield,' one of them growled in a long-suffering voice. His name was Bomber. Almost entirely bald except for a spine of coloured spikes which stuck out from his head, he looked like a cross between a clown and a rooster.

'I don't care.' Dr Plaxton was a shade paler, and actually shaking. 'I'm not having five thousand hours' work put at risk by a pair of – of freaks who never take a bath.'

'Don't need to bath,' Bomber objected, glancing at his repulsive companion, Brig. 'We sweats regular.'

Dr Plaxton's thin, angular face contorted as she struggled

to speak. There was a mist of perspiration on her pale forehead. 'Out!'

'Now look here, lady——'

'Get,' Dr Plaxton shrilled, losing all composure, '*out!*'

Napier stepped forward. 'I'll move it. You'd better go,' he told Bomber and Brig. They hesitated, exchanging sour looks, and then shambled to the exit, cannoning off the door as they went.

Dr Plaxton watched them go, breathing hard through pinched nostrils.

'They'll complain to Atlan,' Napier said warningly, positioning the shield across the photonic drive thrust tube.

'What the hell do I care.' Dr Plaxton took up a piece of apparatus and examined it angrily. 'How I came to be mixed up with a bunch of psychopathic killers . . .' She shook her head, bereft of words.

'It was your decision, Dr Plaxton.' Napier shrugged his narrow shoulders. 'And one that you were happy to make at the time, as I recall.'

'That was three years ago, Napier,' Dr Plaxton said coldly, moving back to the control panel. She was calmer now. Forget those stupid imbeciles. They weren't important. Her work was all that mattered.

Napier looked at the photonic drive under its protective canopy. For a new and revolutionary concept in spacedrives it was deceptively basic and ordinary in appearance, even fragile. Harnessing light as a power source . . . so beautifully simple, yet with the supreme advantage that it could draw its 'fuel' from the light of the stars, no matter how faint or distant.

'Everything's ready for the test, Dr Plaxton. Do you fetch him or shall I?'

'I'll go.'

She detested seeing Atlan in his lair – she detested seeing him at all – but today everything was her responsibility. Nothing must go wrong.

His quarters were in their usual disgusting state. Atlan

and the rest of his obnoxious breed were smoking some foul leaf that filled the air with pungent green smoke. There must have been twenty or more of them, of both sexes, lying about on the mounds of cushions, drinking, gambling, pawing each other. Sprawled before the television monitor, the huge brutish form of their leader had his tattooed arm around a sluttish creature with tangled black hair to her waist and most of her bosom showing through the loosely-stitched animal skins of her costume.

Feeling soiled even to be here, Dr Plaxton stepped over bodies and the congealed remains of food weeks old. Atlan saw her coming, pulled the girl roughly to him, kissed her on the mouth and shoved her aside, stretching his arms above his head and pushing a hand through his spiky hair.

His mouth split slowly in a leering grin, his paint-bedecked face creasing in a smile, as the scientist looked down on him, her distaste evident in every prim feature. The drifting smoke stung her eyes.

Silence fell, movement ceased. Everyone waited.

Completely unconcerned by this abrupt focusing of interest, Dr Plaxton announced crisply, 'I'm ready to begin the test on the Mark II drive, Atlan. If you want to see it, you'd better come right away.'

Without waiting for a reply, she turned and went.

Atlan levered himself upright, a hulking giant of a man, and jerked his thumb at the monitor screen. 'Brig – watch that,' he bellowed, then jerked his other thumb towards the cave entrance. 'Bomber, two gooks outside. Fetch. Only don't bend.' Atlan kicked bodies aside as he strode after Dr Plaxton. 'Might wanna talk to them.'

He hawked and spat and lumbered out.

They made it to the concealed entrance in the nick of time. Vila lifted the camouflage tarpaulin aside, Dayna ducked inside, and he quickly followed, pulling the flap down as two Space Rats roared up on their powerful machines. Waiting tensely in the gloom, handguns drawn, they heard the machines tick into silence and then the crunch of heavy footsteps dying away.

Vila made a pantomime of wiping sweat from his brow. Dayna grinned, her teeth flashing in the semi-darkness of the cavern, and holstered her weapon. She said in a low voice, 'The other entrance must lead to their living quarters and probably the spacedrive workshop.'

Vila nodded, peering round at the steel-grey walls which sloped down from the conical roof. 'I'd say that was a fairly safe bet,' he agreed nervously. 'It's about the only thing round here that is safe. This is not a good place to be, Dayna.'

Moving deeper into the chamber, they almost stumbled into a low bulbous shape shrouded under a canvas cover. A pair of landing skids protruded from underneath. Vila pulled the canvas away to reveal the one-piece cockpit dome of a space chopper. There was another identical shape behind.

Vila lowered the canvas and looked meaningfully at Dayna.

'We've seen enough,' she decided, raising the teleport communicator to her lips. 'We'd better report back to the ship and then get the hell out of here.' She thumbed a button. 'Avon, this is Dayna. Do you read?'

His voice came through at once, surprisingly strong and clear, with none of the usual space static. 'Go ahead, Dayna.'

'Orac was right. This is where the new spacedrives come from. We've found two space choppers and we think the workshop is in the west cliff. We're ready for teleport,' Dayna said, winking at Vila.

'Teleport is out of commission.'

Avon's voice sounded so blandly indifferent that at first Vila didn't get it. Then he did. He stabbed the button on his own communicator and said in a hoarse frantic whisper, 'What do you mean, out of commission!'

'Not working, Vila,' came the brisk reply. 'Keep your heads down. We'll be in touch. Out.'

The communicator went dead. Vila stared at it, bug-eyed. His shoulders slumped. He seemed utterly lost and forlorn.

Dayna beckoned. 'Come on, we've got to find somewhere safe to wait.' She moved further into the gleaming chamber, seeking a suitable hiding-place.

Vila thought he'd found one. On his knees, he squirmed under the canvas cover. 'Maybe we could hide in here,' he said, his voice muffled. Crawling in, he cracked his head on a rounded probe-like projection and winced. 'Wonder what this thing does?' he muttered irritably. He crawled out again, deciding that he'd rather be with Dayna than on his own.

'Tell you what *this* does, gook.'

Vila gazed glassily up the tarnished barrel of an ancient carbine, held in the hairy paws of a Space Rat with a hideously painted face.

'It goes bang,' said Bomber, nostrils flared. 'And you go splat.'

Tarrant swept the portable radiation detector round in an arc, studying the gauge read out. The red needle jumped and quivered. 'There's another one.'

Avon cautiously led the way along the rutted track leading to the Space Rats' base. The track rose slightly and then dropped away, out of sight, to the compound littered with rusting machinery.

After a dozen paces they came upon a surveillance camera concealed in a thorn thicket, and left the track, skirting round behind it.

Avon nodded at the camera and grinned at the other two. 'Useful,' he said in an undertone. 'Save us having to provide a marker for the grenade.'

He unzipped an arm pouch, took out a small circular object with a round flat base, and handed it to Soolin. She held it up as Avon raised the antenna on the miniature radio transmitter. He turned a dial and pressed a black button, and the timer in the stick grenade whirred and clicked. 'Okay, it's primed,' he told her.

The blonde girl crouched and tossed the grenade onto the track, where it rolled into a rut.

Keeping to the rocks, the three of them circled round to a position overlooking the rocks and the cliff-face. They had barely settled down to watch when Vila and Dayna emerged from one of the doors and were marched at gunpoint to the other concealed entrance. The Space Rat prodded them inside and went in after them.

Avon lowered the magni-viewer, a sardonic smile lurking at the corners of his mouth. 'We'll be ready to attack by the time Vila tells them that we're still on the ship.'

'I hope so, Avon,' Soolin murmured, not looking at him. 'For your sake.'

Chapter Sixteen

His flattened squashed features reflecting the shimmering diamond-shaped patterns from the brightly-glowing thrust tube, Atlan stood with his huge bunched fists resting on his hips, his thick lips moist and slightly parted, a dribble of saliva glinting in the lights.

At the control panel Dr Plaxton edged the graduated slider up another notch until the numerals on the cathode display registered thirty per cent power output. The shriek of the photonic drive increased in pitch, jarring the light globes in their fittings. In the centre of the lead-lined shield, a column of light burned with the intense brilliance of a tiny sun.

Atlan threw out a blunt hand in a gesture of encouragement. 'More!' he bellowed. 'More!'

Napier glanced uneasily at Dr Plaxton as she eased the slider control higher. The numerals flicked rapidly up to fifty per cent. The column of light rose higher, the shriek more piercing.

'Come on – more!' Atlan bawled, craning his thick neck forward, his eyes under the bushy brows sparkling greedily.

'There's no point in overloading the Mark II prototype,' Dr Plaxton said curtly, having to raise her voice to be heard.

Atlan turned on her pugnaciously. 'Without my Space Rats scouring a dozen worlds for your raw materials there'd be no Mark I or Mark II!'

'And without my brains——' Dr Plaxton began.

'Which I might decide I can now do without,' Atlan threatened, curling his lip in a sneer. He went on in a low, dangerous growl, 'So let's see what it can do!'

Her mouth a thin, straight line, the scientist did as she was told. She had little choice.

Napier wiped his palms on his sterile coverall and gritted his teeth as the shrieking whine rose almost to the pain threshold. The thrust tube glowed white, tinged with a blue phosphorescence, too bright to look at with the naked eye. A thin wisp of smoke curled from the centre of the shield, where the column pulsed brilliantly.

'What is it now?' Atlan shouted above the noise, standing nearer the test bed and staring raptly at the body of the photonic drive under its transparent canopy.

'Seventy-five per cent. We *must* close down now, Atlan,' Dr Plaxton pleaded. 'The shield's melting!'

Atlan nodded brusquely. He waited until the crescendo of sound had died away and the thrust column was a dull red before running his hand over the spacedrive's polished surface. So much power! His to command! The thrill he felt was akin to sexual ecstasy.

Stroking it lovingly, he asked in a throaty purr, 'What was the simulated speed?'

Dr Plaxton checked the readout. 'Fifteen,' she answered shortly.

'Time-Distort Fifteen . . . in real-time!' Atlan gloated. 'My Space Rats will be knocking out Federation battle cruisers next.'

'If they've got any left.'

'They have – but not for long,' Atlan smirked, straightening up. He wheeled round, his piggish eyes narrowing until they all but disappeared under the slanting forehead. 'How soon can this be fitted to our space choppers?'

Napier caught Dr Plaxton's eye and looked towards the door. She nodded and he went out.

'Well?' Atlan scowled.

'What's wrong with the Mark I?' Dr Plaxton asked, moving towards the test bed, her hands in the pockets of her coverall. 'It gives your space choppers TeeDee Twelve already.'

'Not as good as Fifteen. No Space Rat likes to put up with second-best.'

'That's all you Space Rats think of,' said Dr Plaxton scathingly, icy contempt in every syllable. 'Violence and speed – speed – speed!'

Atlan folded his rippling tattooed arms and looked down on her. 'As you well know, Dr Plaxton, I'm not a Space Rat, but so long as I give them what they want, then they accept me as their leader.'

'Senseless destruction of Federation ships – you don't even have a plan,' she scoffed.

'Maybe the Space Rats don't have a plan, doctor, but we have, you and me . . .' He raised one bushy eyebrow meaningfully. 'Total control over all the space trade routes.

'I don't want any part of it,' Dr Plaxton snapped. 'All I want to do is develop my spacedrives.'

'Fine.' Atlan nodded and jerked his thumb at the photonic drive. 'So how soon can this one be fitted to our space choppers?'

'It can't.'

Atlan flexed his shoulders and stared down at her. 'Why not?'

'Because this is the only one,' replied Dr Plaxton simply.

'So build more. We've provided you with enough material.'

'I'm a scientist, not a production engineer.' Dr Plaxton turned away, waving her hand carelessly. 'The other reason why it can't be fitted to your space choppers is that it won't fit.'

'Why not?' Atlan snarled. He wanted the Mark II. He must have it.

'The only way to increase the power was to increase the size of the photon generator chamber. This drive unit is intended to be installed in real spacecraft – not toys driven by a bunch of murderous psychopaths.'

'Our agreement——'

'Was that you provide me with resources to continue with my work,' Dr Plaxton said calmly. She turned to face him, her pale eyes cold and steady. 'That's exactly what I have done.'

Atlan took a pace towards her, lacing his thick fingers and bending them back until the joints cracked. His voice was a gentle growl, from the chest, yet filled with infinite menace.

'You will start modification work on this drive now, Dr Plaxton. If you refuse. I shall tell the Space Rats that you are derpiving them of speed.' He smiled with his yellow teeth. 'And I shall let them deal with you in their own fashion.'

Avon raised the corner of a tarpaulin and peered into the gloomy interior. He beckoned with his free hand and Tarrant and Soolin scuttled inside. After a careful look all around, Avon followed them and pulled the flap back into place.

Tarrant was already unloading an assortment of equipment from his shoulder pack. He handed the radiation detector to Avon, who activated it and turned in a slow circle, watching the gauge. Soolin had discovered the space choppers under their gold shrouds. She pointed them out to Avon, who nodded. He aimed the detector at one of the limestone walls and advanced towards it.

'If the readings are anything like accurate . . .' He moved along the rough hewn wall, his eyes on the flickering red needle. '... this should be ...' He halted as the needle swung clear across the gauge. '... the connecting wall.'

Taking three one-foot metal rods from their pouches, Tarrant slotted them together and clipped on the titanium-steel sonic lance head. He connected the assembly to a microminiature power pack and opened out two moulded grips which served as handles.

Kneeling by the wall, Avon gestured to Soolin. 'Watch the entrance.' He set the detector down and scrabbled round on the floor, found a fragment of rock, and inscribed a circle on the rock face. Tarrant knelt beside him. He pressed the sonic lance into the dead centre of the circle, and switched on. There was a throbbing hum, which rose fractionally as the arrow-shaped head began to penetrate the flinty limestone.

Cursing under his breath, Atlan strode angrily into the smoke-filled cavern. Damn that woman! She would carry out those modifications or he'd set the pack on her. If they couldn't have their drug – speed and yet more speed – the Space Rats would become like junkies denied their fix. And they were half-crazy to begin with.

'Brig! Bomber!' he yelled, kicking one of them with his steel-capped boot. 'Get guns. We go into the hills for some hunting!'

The two Space Rats scrambled to their feet. Atlan's eyes narrowed as he noticed they had a new type of handgun stuffed into their belts. He swung round and spotted Vila and Dayna sitting disconsolately in a corner. 'What's this?'

'The gooks,' Bomber grinned vacantly, scratching an armpit.

'Gooks?' Atlan frowned and fingered his chin. 'Don't look like Federation to me.'

'We're not,' Dayna said coldly.

Atlan debated for a moment. Then shrugged his massive shoulders and turned to leave. 'Bend them.'

A dozen pairs of hands reached out eagerly. A spot of good-natured fun to break the monotony. Like tying their legs to two machines and tearing off – in this case, literally – in opposite directions.

Vila and Dayna were dragged across the filthy floor towards the entrance, everyone joining in with snarls of glee. The smell of sweaty bodies was overpowering; Vila gagged, unable to utter a sound. Dayna tried to fight them off, but discovered it was useless. She had seconds to think of something, anything, to get them out of this mess. She cried out:

'Wait! Before you kill us, let us see Dr Plaxton!'

Atlan stiffened. 'Stop!' he roared, and lumbered across to where Dayna and Vila lay bruised and dishevelled, surrounded by the panting, grinning pack. 'You know Dr Plaxton?' he demanded gruffly.

'Sure we do,' said Dayna, watching the huge bear of a man and trying to assess how far she could play him along. All muscle and not much grey matter, she decided.

But Atlan wasn't convinced. He fixed his slitted eyes on Vila, who nodded rapidly like a clockwork toy gone berserk.

'Old friend,' Vila gulped.

'From where, gook?'

Vila cleared his throat. 'Oh . . . way back,' he faltered.

'We were students of the doctor's once,' Dayna stated quietly.

'Studying what?' Atlan asked suspiciously.

Dayna played her trump card. 'Spacedrives,' she told him coolly. 'The photonic drive in particular.'

Atlan reached down and with one hand hauled Vila upright, thrusting his face forward so that his chin touched Vila's chin. Vila quaked, his legs turning to water.

'You too, gook?'

Vila couldn't trust himself to speak. It was all he could do to nod weakly.

'Clever student?'

Vila nodded.

'In that case,' Atlan let him go and Vila nearly fell down again, 'we'd better take you both to see her.' He jerked his thumb towards the entrance.

Dayna got quickly to her feet before he could change his mind and pushed Vila in front of her. Atlan followed. The gooks might be telling the truth or they might not. He'd soon find out.

In the test chamber Dr Plaxton looked up from the control panel, blinking in blank mystification over the top of her apparatus as Dayna rushed forward and warmly embraced her. Not giving the scientist a chance to speak, Dayna gushed with girlish enthusiasm, 'Dr Plaxton, how marvellous to see you again! Remember us – Dayna and Vila? Your best students. We thought we'd never see you again after you left the academy.'

Untangling herself from Dayna's hug, Dr Plaxton stepped back a pace and regarded the two strangers with a mixture of bewilderment and disapproval.

'What is this – some kind of joke?' she demanded tartly. She glared at Atlan. 'I've never seen these people before in my life!'

Dayna laughed gaily. 'Your memory hasn't improved, doctor,' she rushed on, talking fast. 'Remember the time when you forgot where you'd parked your ground car and reported it to the police as having been stolen?'

Dr Plaxton shook her head helplessly. 'I've no idea who these people are,' she informed Atlan, who was tugging reflectively on an ear, still not sure who to believe.

'And this must be your new photonic spacedrive,' Dayna enthused, loping across to the test bed and gazing keenly through the plastic canopy. 'It doesn't look anything like as sophisticated as the prototype we were working on at the academy.' From the corner of her eye she saw Atlan glance sharply at Dr Plaxton. Dayna nodded sagely to herself. 'Of course, that's only to be expected, having to work under these conditions . . .'

Dr Plaxton raised her hands, appealing to Atlan. 'Look, I can't remember who these people are!' she protested.

'Can't or won't?' Atlan growled, twisting his thick lips. His eyes flicked back and forth between Vila and Dayna. 'Could you two work on the development of the photonic drive?' he asked craftily.

Vila made a dumb show of not being sure, but Dayna answered without a moment's hesitation. 'Of course.'

'This is my project!' Dr Plaxton shrilled, thumping the panel.

Atlan gave her his leering, yellow-toothed grin. 'Not for much longer, it seems,' he sneered.

Dr Plaxton was white to the lips. 'You'd do that,' she raged, marching up to him with clenched fists, 'after all I've done for you and your bunch of killers!'

As she moved from the control panel Vila's attention was caught by a section of limestone wall between the sound-proofing baffles ranged round the room. For a second he thought it was crumbling away. He looked again. It *was* crumbling away! Signalling frantically with his eyebrows to Dayna, he indicated this strange phenomenon by swivelling his eyes to and fro. She saw it too, and gave an almost imperceptible nod.

Atlan said bluntly, 'I'd do a lot more than that if you prove to be of no further use to me, doctor.'

Dayna's thoughts were racing. Any minute Atlan would be bound to notice the crumbling wall. She had to stage a diversion. Moving swiftly to the control panel, she said in a loud, brisk voice, 'First we'd better see if that drive is up to standard.' She started pressing buttons at random. 'How do I start it?'

'No!' Dr Plaxton spun round. 'Leave that alone!'

'We have to know how it performs,' Dayna insisted, undeterred.

'No——'

'Start it up!' Atlan commanded in a tone that implied it would be unwise to refuse.

Dr Plaxton breathed audibly through her nostrils and strode to the control panel. Pushing Dayna aside, she went quickly through the operating sequence and nudged the slider along the graduated scale. The spacedrive emitted a low pulsing whine. After a few seconds the thrust tube began to glow. Vila edged out of Atlan's line of sight and risked a glance at the wall. Now there was a sizeable hole there, and then a hand appeared, breaking off chunks of limestone which thudded to the floor.

Vila darted forward, his voice thin with urgency. 'We need more power!'

'Why?' Atlan boomed.

'Well . . .' Vila smiled and spread his hands. 'If we're to carry out a proper assessment . . .'

Thankfully the mounting whine of the spacedrive completely blotted out the noise of the collapsing wall. And both Atlan and Dr Plaxton had their eyes glued to the brilliantly glowing column of light, giving Avon, Tarrant and Soolin just the opportunity they needed to climb through the enlarged hole, weapons drawn. They spread out in a semi-circle.

'What do you think of it?' Atlan asked Dayna, a smirk of pride disfiguring his squat features.

'Very nice,' said Avon nonchalantly, smiling a slow devilish smile. His finger tightened on the trigger as Atlan whirled round. 'It'll be even nicer if you keep quite still.'

Chapter Seventeen

Face beaming with relief, Vila started across the chamber to welcome his fellow crew members. Avon gestured him back angrily – the idiot was walking straight into the line of fire.

Too late.

Atlan saw his chance and took it. For a big man he was amazingly quick. In three gigantic strides he was across the chamber and had dived through the door before anyone could get a clear shot.

'Tarrant!' Avon pointed and the young pilot charged after him.

In the corridor he glimpsed Atlan disappearing through another door and yelling at the top of his lungs for reinforcements. Tarrant flattened himself against the wall and unclipped a smoke grenade from his belt. Inside it sounded like pandemonium as Atlan roused his men. There was a rush of feet and mingled oaths, like a drunken army of louts out for blood. Tarrant tossed the grenade inside and slammed the door shut in Atlan's face.

An explosion of coughing and wheezing broke out as Tarrant ran back to the test chamber and slammed and bolted the door.

Already Dayna had closed the photonic drive down, the tube a dull red. Avon beckoned to Tarrant to help him to remove the protective canopy.

'Take me with you — please!' Dr Plaxton begged. She looked round wildly at the distant sounds of hammering and shouting from along the corridor. 'I'm finished here. *Please!*'

'We take you *and* your photonic drive,' Avon said crisply. 'Now show us how to move it.'

Atlan staggered back against the wall, tears streaming from his eyes. The chamber was filled with dense, choking fumes. He dropped to his knees where he was able to suck in a lungful of air.

Nearby he saw Bomber crouched over, vomiting. Atlan lumbered to his feet and wiped his eyes. The smoke was slowly clearing. He grasped Bomber by the scruff of the neck and lifted him upright. Dayna's handgun was still in his belt. Atlan seized it and aimed at the door. The power of the weapon was a revelation. One short burst, a fizzing blue streak of energy, and the neutron bolt tore the heavy door off its hinges.

Stepping into the corridor, Atlan urged his men in pursuit. Looking up, he saw Napier creeping towards the outside entrance. Atlan fondled the handgun lovingly. Slowly and deliberately he raised it, aimed and fired, cutting Napier in half.

The door to the test chamber was barred. Atlan cleared a space around him and aimed a bolt at the door. A moment later he burst through the sheared woodwork and skidded to a halt, shoulders hunched, his eyes bloodshot with rage.

There was a gaping hole in the chamber wall and the test bed was empty.

With a snarl of fury, Atlan charged out, clearing a path through the Space Rats like a bull through a flock of sheep.

Avon and Soolin covered the concealed entrance as the others lugged the spacedrive across the compound. Vila was complaining, as usual, about having to do his share of the donkey work. If Avon thought he was going to carry it all the way back to the ship, then Avon had another think coming.

His face brightened as he saw a half-track transporter parked by the entrance. The very thing! The smile evaporated as three Space Rats leapt out of the cab, armed to their rotting yellow teeth, and began spraying fire all around. Vila dropped his corner of the spacedrive and hit the ground, nose first.

Down on one knee, Avon took his time and picked off the driver. Soolin's hand was a blur as she aimed and fired in one continuous movement, hitting the other two so quickly it seemed like a single shot. Avon turned to her admiringly and caught a glimpse of something from the corner of his eye.

'Soolin!'

The blonde girl whipped round, firing from the hip, and hit the Space Rat who had just emerged from the camouflaged entrance dead in the centre of his slanting forehead. The headless body tottered a few paces, spouting blood like a fountain, and fell splayed out, a fat black X on the grey chalk.

While Soolin kept watch, Avon supervised the loading of the spacedrive onto the transporter. Dr Plaxton, her greying hair hanging in wisps over her pale forehead, climbed into the cab and started the engine.

In a muttered aside to Tarrant, Avon said, 'She's a little too good to trust.'

Tarrant lifted the tailboard and slotted in the locking pins. 'When was trust a problem for you?' he asked tersely. 'Anyway, we need her – she's the only one who can operate this thing.'

A fusillade of carbine fire echoed across the compound. Vila and Dayna jumped into the cab while Avon and Tarrant heaved themselves onto the back of the transporter. The motor roared and the transporter jerked into motion.

'Soolin!' Avon yelled.

The blonde girl was slowly retreating, still firing from the hip. As the half-track gathered speed she turned and ran and was swept up by Avon and Tarrant's reaching arms. Then with the three of them hanging on to the photonic drive to prevent it bouncing about, the transporter rattled up the rutted track, heading for the open countryside. Behind them they saw the Space Rats burst from the concealed entrance, with the huge form of Atlan at their head. As the transporter topped the shallow rise they saw him leap onto a machine and kick it into life, gesticulating to the others to mount up.

Avon took the miniature radio transmitter from the equipment pack and raised the antenna. Bracing himself against the tailboard, he watched the track keenly, his thumb hovering over the black button. Above the rumble and clank of the transporter he could hear the throaty roar of several machines, closing rapidly.

The transporter passed a TV camera in a thorn thicket and Avon spotted the grenade lying in one of the ruts where Soolin had tossed it. A moment later it was out of sight as they turned a bend. He couldn't see Atlan or any of the others, but he could guess their position from the sound of the engines. Counting silently to himself, Avon waited for the precise instant and pressed the button.

The result was spectacular and instantaneous.

A ragged sheet of orange flame spurted skywards, tossing the disassembled bits and pieces of a man and machine high into the air, and they heard the gritty crump of the explosion reverberating flatly across the dead bleached landscape.

'That should slow them up,' Tarrant remarked, straining to hear the sound of engines. He couldn't.

'Up being the operative word,' Avon commented with a lift of an eyebrow.

Soolin wasn't enjoying the shuddering, jolting ride one bit. Hanging on to the spacedrive, she said through gritted teeth, 'I'm never going to complain about *Scorpio* again. This is not a comfortable way to travel.'

Chapter Eighteen

Tarrant eased back in his seat and flexed his hands. 'Primary orbit achieved,' he said with a boyish grin. Everyone started to unfasten their straps, Dayna helping Dr Plaxton with hers.

'Slave!' Avon alerted the computer. 'Activate all sensory systems and set course three-nine-zero at maximum drive. I'll give you a navigation program once we're clear of this planetary system.'

'At once, Master.'

Avon punched up a scan pattern on the main screen and studied it with a pensive frown.

'You think they'll come after us in those space choppers?' Tarrant queried.

'I don't think, I know.' Avon answered briefly.

Soolin wandered up to the flight control position, holding two identical components, one in either hand. They were small copper coils, with co-axial leads trailing from them as if they'd been torn out of some other equipment.

She held them up. 'That depends on how important these are.'

Dr Plaxton stepped across to examine them. 'Where did you get these?'

'Souvenirs from those two space choppers,' Soolin said innocently, an impish smile lurking at the corners of her mouth.

The scientist's austere face softened and she gave a rasping chuckle. 'They won't be able to move an inch without those.'

Everyone looked up as Slave said in a tone of apology, 'I am sorry to have to report, Master, that three Federation pursuit ships are approaching on an intercept of zero-three-zero-zero-seven.'

Avon aligned the scan to the new co-ordinates and everyone gazed anxiously at the screen as three red shapes with swept-back fins appeared. They were Federation all right.

'What's the range, Dayna?' Avon rapped out.

'Two hundred thousand.'

Slave interposed with some fresh information. 'Their signals traffic indicates that they think we're from Caspar.'

Avon stared bleakly at the scanner screen. Just their rotten luck to be mistaken for Space Rats. 'The state our main drive's in, we'll be in range of their cannons within an hour,' he said grimly.

'What's the matter with your main drive?' asked Dr Plaxton sharply.

Tarrant grinned wryly. 'It's a museum piece.'

'Standard fibre-optic control connections?'

'Very standard,' Avon told her, not taking his eyes off the screen.

Dr Plaxton paused. On the screen the pursuit ships could be clearly seen getting nearer. She said briskly, 'In that case, why not let me install the photonic drive now? One burst from that and you'd put a lot of distance between us and those ships.'

Avon looked at Tarrant and then at Dr Plaxton. 'How long would it take?'

'I should estimate . . . about fifty minutes.'

'Dayna?' Avon said.

The girl was checking readouts at the navigation desk. She glanced over her shoulder. 'If it's to be done it'll have to be done in forty-five.'

All eyes were on Dr Plaxton. It was a hairline decision to make, but the survival of the ship and everyone on board depended on it. To their immense relief the scientist nodded. 'Right. You'll have to find a way of pressurising the interior of your main drive tube. I'll need help to get the photonic drive in position and then you can leave me to it.'

Dayna set the central digital display on countdown. 'Forty-four minutes and thirty-five seconds and counting . . .'

Dr Plaxton leaned over the thrust tube and expertly threaded and clamped one of the fibre-optic connections to the junction panel. The work was second nature to her. She had been weaned on the old chemical drives. Nasty, temperamental beasts.

This old bucket wasn't much better. The sleek, gleaming shape of the photonic drive looked oddly out of place in the blackened and scarred drive chamber. But once connected up, it would give the ship an incredible top speed of Time-Distort Fifteen – faster even than the latest Federation pursuit craft.

Dayna's voice came over the headset, sounding anxious. 'Less than two minutes, doctor . . .'

Dr Plaxton moistened her dry lips and said over the throat mike, 'Nearly finished. Just the main ignition controls.' Using the tweezers, she selected the next terminal and guided it into the digital-coded slot.

On the flight deck the crew were gathered tensely round the communication console. The Federation ships were now much bigger and sharper on the screen, their pointed prows catching the light of distant stars.

Vila could hardly bear to look. He had his hand across his eyes and kept peering through his fingers, hoping that the next time he looked the ships would have magically vanished. But they were still there, getting nearer, looming larger by the second.

Avon was watching the digits flicking by on the display. 'One minute precisely, doctor.'

Dr Plaxton clamped another terminal in place. 'Two more connections. Not long now.' She reached for the next but last terminal, fumbled the tweezers, and dropped them. She heard them clatter and groped blindly under the thrust tube.

Seated in the pilot's position, Tarrant raised his eyes from the bank of instruments. 'They're in range,' he reported tersely.

'Time's up, doctor,' Avon said into the communicator.

'Almost done,' came the reply.

Soolin was watching the screen. Sharp-eyed, she saw the tiny flash of light and called out, 'Plasma bolt fired!'

'That gives us thirty seconds,' Dayna said, biting her lip.

Over the communicator they heard Dr Plaxton say, 'Just one more terminal to——'

Avon cut her off in mid-sentence and swung into the co-pilot's seat. He started punching buttons and scanning readouts, his face a stiff, expressionless mask.

'What are you doing?' Tarrant demanded uncertainly.

'Switching in the main drive circuits.'

Dayna's eyes snapped wide in shocked disbelief. 'You can't do that!' she protested hoarsely. 'The drive will fire as soon as she makes the final connection.'

'Fifteen seconds to impact,' Soolin said thinly.

Avon threw the last switch, completing the firing sequence. His voice was drab and cold. 'If we don't outrun that bolt the ship's had it and everyone on board.' He looked at the others, his eyes hooded, unfathomable. 'She's dead either way.'

'Ten seconds and counting,' Soolin chanted, watching the luminous fireball of the plasma bolt swelling on the screen. 'Nine . . . eight . . . seven . . . six . . .'

In the drive chamber Dr Plaxton guided the final terminal towards the junction panel. With a steady, nerveless hand she pushed it home and secured the clamp. Instantly the photonic drive came alive. A beam of raw energy illuminated the thrust tube to an intense pulsating whiteness. The shrill whine ascended to full power.

Inches away from the tube, Dr Plaxton saw her hands turn black and shrivel. Then she saw nothing more as the brilliant light melted her eyeballs. She tried to open her mouth to scream but her face didn't exist any more. Her head became a charred knob, like a shrunken pygmy's, and soon there was nothing left except a heap of ashes.

The flight deck was in chaos, loose equipment scattered everywhere, from the effect of the tremendous acceleration.

Strapped to a crash-couch, Soolin could hardly believe the evidence of her own eyes as the plasma bolt shrank to a tiny pinpoint of light. If they could outpace that, they could outpace anything.

Avon was shaking his head at the spinning dials in front of him. Incredible. *Scorpio* was faster than *Liberator* had been. With this kind of power they could really start to hit the Federation hard. Where it hurt. *And* get clean away to fight another day.

'At least now we can outrun the opposition,' he said with grim satisfaction, glancing round at the rest of the crew. 'That should make you all feel happier.'

Dayna looked far from happy. 'What about Dr Plaxton?' she said stonily.

Everyone was watching Avon. He met their stares without a flicker of emotion on his lean, saturnine face. 'Who?'